BARRY CRUMP

ARTY AND THE FOX

Illustrated by Pat Trembeth

BOOKS BY BARRY CRUMP

A Good Keen Man (1960)*
Hang on a Minute Mate (1961)*
One of Us (1962)*
There and Back (1963)*
Gulf (1964) – *now titled* Crocodile Country*
Scrapwagon (1965)
The Odd Spot of Bother (1967)
No Reference Intended (1968)
Warm Beer and Other Stories (1969)
A Good Keen Girl (1970)
Bastards I have Met (1971)
Fred (1972)
Shorty (1980)
Puha Road (1982)
The Adventures of Sam Cash (1985)
Wild Pork and Watercress (1986)*
Bullock Creek (1989)*
The Life and Times of a Good Keen Man (1992)*
Gold and Greenstone (1993)*

** currently (1994) in print*

BARRY CRUMP

Barry Crump wrote his first book, *A Good Keen Man*, in 1960. It became an immediate best-seller, as did numerous other books which followed. His most famous and best-loved New Zealand character is Sam Cash, who features in *Hang on a Minute Mate*, Crump's second book. His first two books have sold over 400,000 copies and continue to sell at an amazing rate, some 30 years later. Two other Crump books feature Sam Cash, *One of Us* and *There and Back*; both are very entertaining and highly successful, and have been re-released due to popular demand.

Crump began his working life as a professional hunter, culling deer and pigs in some of the ruggedest country in New Zealand. After the runaway success of his first book, he pursued many diverse activities, including gold-mining, radio talkback, white-baiting, television presenting, crocodile shooting, acting and numerous others. His face is familiar to all New Zealanders through a series of motor-vehicle commercials which have won world-wide acclaim.

He is listed in *Who's Who in New Zealand* as author, of no fixed abode. He is currently somewhere in the South Island of New Zealand doing what he fondly calls research. He has contracted one of his books, *Wild Pork and Watercress*, to be made into a full-feature movie. In 1990 he wrote *The Life and Times of a Good Keen Man*, another in the vivid style that has enthralled his readers for three decades. This is the author's own story, a fascinating account of the remarkable life of one of New Zealand's truly great characters. As to classifying his occupation, Crump insists that he always has been, and always will be, a Kiwi bushman, but perhaps these days 'itinerant scribe' would be more appropriate.

He was awarded the MBE in 1994 for service to literature.

ARTY AND THE FOX
© Barry Crump 1994

Published in 1994 by
Moa Beckett Publishers Limited
28 Poland Road, Glenfield
PO Box 100-749, North Shore Mail Centre, Auckland 1330

Reprinted 1994

Printed by McPherson's Printing Group, Australia

ISBN 1-86958-080-X

All rights reserved. No part of this publication may be reproduced, stored in a retrieval system or transmitted in any form or by any means, electronic, mechanical, photocopying, recording or otherwise, without the prior permission in writing of the publisher.

CONTENTS

AJAX

The Chickens

THE WORLD turned around. As the part of it we're interested in rolled into the sunlight the snowy peaks along the Turnbull Range were tinted pink. For a few moments Pyke's Peak looked like a huge ice-cream in a black cone. As the light spread down across the bushed mountainsides, it gradually lit up the roofs and roads of a small country town called Matea (pop. 1675), on the banks of the Turnbull River, until the sun struck diamonds on the dewdrops in the spider-webs on the fence outside Arty Brown's place on the edge of town, and lit up the splendid array of junk along Arty's fences and around the sides and back of his big shed. We won't show you what's inside that shed just yet, some things take a bit of leading up to.

You could see a concrete mixer, a steam cleaner and an obsolete water-blasting machine and three old tractors and a 1968 Bedford truck with no motor and the deck piled high with big rolls of copper wire. In one corner there was a trailer and a baler and an old wooden boat, a set of chain-harrows and a broken conveyor-belt. Along the fence from that there were drums and crates and netting and gates and coils of used wire rope. There were bales and rails and pipes and pails and dozens of plastic containers.

There were wheels and rims and tyres and tins and stacks of buckled timber, machines and beams and cans for cream and boxes of rusty nails. It would take several sessions of prolonged browsing to take it all in. This impressive conglomeration covered most of Arty's two-acre paddock. A dented grey car, which was badly in need of a coat of paint, was parked in the driveway beside the house. There was an old green three-ton truck down by the shed that looked as though it might be still operational.

Arty's wife Carol was a cheerful and tolerant soul, but she'd had to insist that auctions were out of bounds to Arty. It had become too outrageous. They had three kids and Carol was a teacher at the Matea primary school.

Arty was an optimist. Medium height, fair hair, bony, always wore jeans and boots and woollen shirts. He was about forty, getting a bit late for a man to make a success of himself at something, according to some who knew him.

Arty would have loved to be a dealer but he never got to do much dealing. Perhaps it was the kinds of stuff he tried to deal in. The result of his efforts was this impressive conglomeration of junk that Arty had bought cheap and was still waiting to 'flick off'.

There'd been complaints from time to time about his place being an eyesore and lowering property values in the area. People regarded him as a bit of a joke, but one of these days some of this stuff was going to become valuable, then they'd be laughing on the other side of their faces. In the meantime he'd been forbidden to attend any more auctions under threat of divorce, which had been successful in partly reducing the influx of junk onto the place.

The main snag about all this stuff of Arty's was that if anyone did want something he had there, he found it very difficult to charge them for it, or even put a price on it. He couldn't remember what he'd paid for most of it. He could buy the stuff all right, but, let's face it, when it came to selling anything – he was hopeless. In fact someone had once described Arty as 'disaster-prone'.

Arty had one friend who hadn't given up on him. Joe Buckner. They'd met through their wives, who'd been close friends since they were at school together in Danby. Joe was more of an outdoor type than Arty. He'd been a shearer, a dozer-driver, a miner, a fisherman. He was driving trucks mostly these days.

Arty was always on the go, Joe was more laid-back, and the informal partnership that had happened out of the blue suited both of them.

Joe had met his wife Helen at the timber yard, where she worked in the office, and she'd taken an instant shine to him. Joe was bowled over. Helen was one of those people who were good-looking without seeming to be aware of it. Tall and slim with long red hair. She was a good wife and a conscientious worker. Her only drawback was the fact that she had a hell of a temper on her, and once she got her dander up she took a lot of settling down again. Even her boss at the timber yard was a bit cautious of her. Joe and Helen had no children and lived half a mile from Arty and Carol's place.

Arty and Joe had been engaged in various money-making schemes over the years, none of which had turned out quite as expected. In fact they'd mostly cost more money than they'd made. They'd got a contract a while back to remove seventy-five Ks of obsolete telephone line. It cost them dearly – they couldn't sell the stuff. It was still in Arty's yard, waiting for the price of copper to go up. They'd bought 4,000 cigarette lighters real cheap because some of them were slightly faulty. Some of them were slightly faulty, the rest wouldn't work at all. They were still in their boxes stashed in Arty's shed. They got themselves a cheap refrigerated van and bought whitebait on the coast for twenty dollars a kilo and carted it over the hill to Danby, where the most they could get for it was twenty-two dollars a kilo.

Their profits didn't pay for the gas they used. And so on.

Arty drove a local taxi part-time and did other casual work around the town, and Joe drove trucks or tractors whenever the work came up, but it was always temporary these days. If their wives hadn't been working they wouldn't have been able to keep going, and they were always keen to make a bit of extra money.

Carol and Helen could hardly be blamed for having become somewhat sceptical about these enterprises, and Joe and Arty had learned to be discreet about how much they took them into their confidence. Their last two major projects had come badly undone, one after the other, and yet no one could have predicted the way it happened, except maybe with the cabbages.

The first was the chickens. Arty scored an incubator for a hundred and fifty dollars, a bargain in anyone's language, it was worth about three thousand dollars if you had to make one up from scratch. That's if you were into incubating large numbers of chickens.

"What are you going to do with it?" said Joe, examining the dismantled incubator on the back of the truck outside his place.

"We can breed chickens," said Arty enthusiastically. "The bloke I got it off told me all about it. There's good money in it. He was all set up to make a packet!"

"What made him give it up then?"

"His missus. She's allergic to chooks. They bring her out in rashes."

Joe raised an eyebrow at this. "So you're going to breed chickens," he said.

"I'll need help, Joe. We can go halves. We can breed five hundred chickens at a time with this thing. At twelve weeks old they're worth two dollars fifty each. That's twelve hundred and fifty bucks a batch. Not a bad sideline, eh!"

"Where are we going to keep five hundred chickens for three months?" Joe wanted to know.

"On my place," said Arty, spreading his hands. "We just have to feed them there and they'll hang around."

"I hope you're right about that," said Joe. "Hell, five hundred chooks running loose around the place! I don't like to think about it."

"No worries," Arty assured him. "They'll still be chickens, and chickens don't stray from where they're fed. I've checked up on it."

"Checked? How?"

"I've asked quite a few people about it. Some of them have had chooks for years, and they all say the same, feed 'em there and they'll stay there. You never see chickens running away from the hen, do you?"

"I hope you're right," repeated Joe, "but I suppose it's worth giving it a go. We've got nothing much else going on."

They cleared an area in Arty's shed and assembled the incubator.

We promised to show you what's in that shed of Arty's and this would be a good opportunity. There were shelves down both sides and a long bench across the back wall beneath two big windows, and a great stack of stuff up the middle of the floor. The shelves and bench were chocka with stuff of every description. Unlike the things scattered around outside, most of the stuff in the shed was unused, but you could hardly call it new. It was mostly obsolete but not yet antique. A lot of it was stuff that hadn't been around since pocket knives had spikes for picking stones out of horses' hooves and kids were being told never to put water on a burn.

There were boxes of toe and heel plates for leather boots and shoes. There were mechanical car-jacks, black wall telephones, electric motors, pressure cookers, sugar dispensers that used to be used in restaurants, hot water bottles, tyre pumps, coils of hemp rope, cartons of parts for things like hand lawnmowers and hand-wringers. There were methylated-spirit toasters, kerosene cookers, petrol soldering-irons, white-spirit blow torches and oil lamps. There were bow-saw frames, porcelain insulators and windmill parts. That's just glancing along one wall.

The other side of the shed was what could loosely be called the stationery department. The shelves were loaded with misprinted exercise books and out-of-date calendars. Rolls of gift-wrap paper with designs no one wanted, pencils with green lead, plastic photograph frames, maintenance handbooks for not-quite-antique cars and motor bikes, meat thermometers, magnifying glasses, tea towels, stationery trays, pottery seconds and gadgets to hold tennis balls on the sides of beer mugs.

Up the middle of the floor was an array of black-and-white television sets, knitting machines, ash-tray stands, stereograms, glory boxes, sewing machines, wooden kitset furniture, bundles of army blankets, air force uniforms and printed cardboard cartons, as well as bales of gloves, made in China and too small for Kiwi hands.

That's just a cross-section of the stuff Arty had in his shed, and every item was the relic of a scheme or dream that Arty had believed was going to give him the break he needed to "put him in the money".

It was into this warehouse of unwanted merchandise that Arty and Joe introduced their chicken-breeding operation, and when they'd got the incubator working, they bought five hundred and fifty-two fertilised eggs. Forty-six dozen eggs. They had to get them from several different poultry farms, two of them more than a hundred Ks away. The eggs were carefully set out on the racks of the incubator which was then plugged in and turned on.

"In three weeks' time they'll all be chickens," said Arty gazing proudly on the rows of eggs gleaming under the warming lights.

"They're going to take some feeding," said Joe.

"Yes," agreed Arty. "We'll have to get in a few sacks of chicken-feed. It'll be a good investment in the long run."

"Well I hope the run isn't too long," said Joe. "We haven't got much money left."

"It'll be worth it," said Arty. "You'll see."

They bought three large sacks of chicken-feed and tipped it into drums with lids, and then they waited.

At this stage Arty's wife had to be let in on it.

"What are you two up to down there in the shed?" she said, pouring them tea.

"We're incubating a few chickens," said Arty.

"Chickens?"

"Yeah, we're going into it commercially. There's big money in it, eh Joe."

"Yep," said Joe with more confidence than he felt.

"How many chickens?" demanded Carol.

"We're only doing five hundred for a start," said Arty.

"Five hundred chickens? Where are we going to keep them?"

"In the yard," said Arty. "We just have to feed them in the yard and they'll stay there. It's only for eight weeks."

"I'm not having them around the house," she warned. "Chickens! What next?"

"Don't worry dear," Arty assured her. "We've got it under control. We'll do all right out of this. You'll see!"

They saw all right. Firstly they saw fifteen little bundles of fluff hatched out one morning. By the next day there were a hundred and sixty, and then they lost count of them. They saw a seething mass of little bundles of fluff happen around them. They saw that some of them were white and some were black, some of them were red and some were speckled, and combinations of all four. They saw them spread out through Arty's shed and around the yard. In, on and under everything everywhere. They saw their drums of chicken-feed go down at an alarming rate.

At first the chickens hung around the yard in the daytime, waiting for their next feed, but at night they had to let them into Arty's shed. Arty covered his most-vulnerable stuff with sheets of polythene and plastic and sacks, but a terrible mess was beginning to happen in the shed. Five hundred chickens . . .

They grew and they flew, and they took no notice of anyone's boundaries. As you approached Arty's place you noticed chickens everywhere, including two or three run over on the road, but it wasn't until feeding time that you could comprehend the full magnitude of it.

As soon as someone approached the chicken-drums with a bucket, chickens would start running and flapping from all directions until you were knee-deep in a squawking, flapping, pecking, scrapping horde of frantic chickens, and hundreds of sparrows flew in and perched on everything above the ground. It was more than a little overwhelming. You'd get a bucket of grain out of a drum and fling a shower of it as far as you could, and the chickens would chase after it, giving you a chance to get the next bucketful out.

When the frenzy died down and the chickens began to disperse around the neighbourhood, there was often a smothered chicken or two lying around on the feathered, muddied-up ground.

Sometimes a chicken would see another chicken running and it would start running too, and a whole wave of running chickens would happen. One poor woman up the road made the mistake of feeding a loaf of stale bread to a roaming bunch of chickens. She ended up with about a hundred of them hanging around. They demolished her garden. No one in the street was game to scrape a plate any more.

Long before the chickens were ready for the table there were complaints coming from all directions. From up the road and down the road and over the back and from the next street behind Arty's place. And then the police paid them a visit, Sergeant Freeman and Cliff James, the Community Constable.

Sergeant Freeman was one of the 'old breed' of policeman. Grizzled and grim-looking, he took no nonsense from criminals, but had been known to kick the odd backside and send youngsters home if the offence wasn't too serious. It had been said of him that his bark was worse than his bite, but that depended on whether he was barking or biting. Arty and Joe had crossed paths with the sergeant a number of times in the past and knew not to push their luck with him too much. He had a knack of getting right to the heart of a matter, and he wanted answers to a number of embarrassing questions:

Where was their permit to run a commercial poultry farm?

What were they going to do about the noise pollution?

Who was going to pay for the damage to the neighbours' gardens and properties?

Who was going to clean up the mess?

The sergeant eventually ordered them to immediately begin reducing the numbers of chickens on the place and said that the police would be considering what charges were to be laid against them.

"We only need another couple of weeks," said Arty, as they watched the policemen depart. "We've got to hang on until then."

"Then what?" said Joe.

"Eh?"

"What do we do with them then?"

"We catch 'em and crate 'em up and send 'em off to the processing factory in Danby."

"How do you reckon we're going to catch them?" enquired Joe.

"We can lock them in the shed when they go in there to roost at night," said Arty.

"What about the ones that don't roost in the shed?" said Joe.

A growing number of chickens had taken to roosting in trees and hedges and orchards around the area. More than a dozen of them were camping at night in the apple tree by Arty's house.

"We can lure them into the shed with grain and shut them in," said Arty, spreading his hands as though it was the most simple thing on earth.

"I sure hope so," said Joe, who was beginning to sense another disaster coming up.

By this time they were so short of money for chicken-feed that they were scrounging it day by day. The chickens had got to know Joe's ute and as he drove up with the day's chicken-feed the chickens came running up the road in an hysterical rabble to meet him. By the time he reached Arty's gate he was crawling along in low gear surrounded by a sea of squawking flapping chickens, with a dozen or two perched all over the ute.

"That's it!" said Carol to Arty. "Either those fowls go or I do. I've had enough of it. It's too embarrassing!"

"But dear," said Arty. "They're not quite ready for the market yet. In another couple of weeks . . ."

"No," she said. "I want them out of here right now, or I'm going. And that's that! It's got so I'm ashamed to put my head out the door. I ran over one of them with the car this morning, right in front of the Johnson kids. I'm not putting up with it!"

She meant it. Arty got a buyer from the processing factory over at Danby to come and put a price on the chickens.

"They're not heavy enough," said the buyer. "And they're not uniform. I'll give you a dollar-thirty a head, delivered at the factory."

He wouldn't negotiate, that was his top price. Arty and Joe decided to trap the chickens in the shed and crate them up, which was easier said than done. It took them an hour and a half to catch sixteen chickens and put them in cardboard boxes with air-holes punched in them. They'd chase a dozen chickens into a corner and be lucky to grab one of them. There were panicking chickens all over the place and they had to poke them down off the shelves and rafters with a broom. They went up to the house for a cup of tea because the noise and the heat and the smell of ammonia was getting to them.

"Well we've got most of 'em in there, anyway," said Arty.

"Yeah," said Joe, "but at this rate the ones we've caught are going to die of old age before we can catch the rest of them."

"We need a way to catch them in bulk," said Arty.

They found a way. They strung a four-inch gill-net across the shed and chased the chickens into it. That way they caught two hundred and fifty and crated them up. That night they went down with a torch and caught another eighty while they were perched asleep around the shed. And next morning they consigned 350 chickens off to the factory in Danby. Thirty-five boxes of them.

There were still a fair few chickens hiding behind stuff in the shed, they could hear them cheeping, so they opened the doors and let them out to join the ones still outside.

By this time Carol had packed up the kids and gone off to Joe and Helen's place. She wasn't coming back until every chicken was gone. She was concerned about being able to hold her head up among the neighbours ever again.

The next day Arty and Joe lured about a hundred chickens into the shed with the last of the chicken-feed and caught and crated most of them and sent them off the next morning. Nine chickens came to be fed the next day. They caught six of them with the fishing net and Joe shot two of the others with an air rifle. The other one escaped over the back fence into the neighbour's place. There was no doubt a few others were still scattered around the district.

With the chickens gone and Carol not quite ready to come home yet, Arty's place was eerily quiet. There were feathers and chicken manure everywhere and the ground was trodden into mud wherever it was a bit damp, and the whole outfit stank of chickens, especially in the shed. This wasn't helped by the fact that a few chickens had got stuck in behind things in the shed and died there.

They'd sold 445 chickens at a dollar-thirty each. Under six hundred dollars. The chicken-feed had cost more than that, and they still had possible damages and legal charges to worry about.

No, the chickens couldn't be called a success by any stretch of the imagination. Arty and Joe were running true to form.

The Cabbages

The fowl manure had played havoc with a lot of Arty's 'good stuff' in his shed. They'd scraped off, shaken out and shovelled up about half a ton of it and, for want of somewhere to put it, wheelbarrowed it out and scattered it on the ground behind the shed. And that's what gave rise to Arty's next inspiration.

"Cabbages, Joe! I don't know why I didn't think of it before. I've always been good at growing things, and we've got all this ground and it's already manured! We've only got to dig it up and plant it in cabbages!"

"Cabbages?" said Joe, doing a quick flit through the possibilities of coming undone growing cabbages.

"Not just any old cabbages," said Arty. "These'll be organically grown cabbages. Everyone's getting into organically grown stuff these days."

"What is organic, anyway?"

"No chemical manures or sprays. Everything natural. They can't get enough of it! It's the right time of year for planting them, too!"

"Well, I can't see any harm in growing a few cabbages," said Joe slowly. "At least they're not going to escape all over the district on us."

Joe had no idea how wrong he was about that.

They spent a day and a half fixing up an old rotary hoe that Arty had stored in some blackberry bushes in the corner of his paddock. Then they cleared the stuff off about a quarter of an acre behind the shed and hoed it up. Joe finished the hoeing while Arty made a trip to Danby and came back with the tray of Joe's ute filled with boxes of cabbage seedlings. He'd bought every cabbage seedling he could find in the city.

They marked out the rows and planted the seedlings eighteen inches apart, and used just over half of them. So they planted the extra ones in between. Then they rigged up a sprinkler system and spread four bags of blood-and-bone they swapped a tractor tyre for. It was looking good, all the rows of cabbage seedlings standing up straight and leafy in the loose damp ground. Even Carol cautiously admitted that it looked nice and tidy.

Now when Arty said he was good at growing things he wasn't kidding. Those cabbages really grew for him. He spent hours in the garden every day at first, teasing up the ground around each plant with a hoe and watering them twice a day.

And they grew. And grew. They grew until they were touching each other and almost knee-high. There wasn't enough space between them. No worries about weeds, the cabbages smothered anything else that tried to grow there.

"Do you think we ought to pull some of them out?" suggested Joe. "Kind of thin 'em out a bit?"

"It's too soon," said Arty expertly. "They're not ready yet, and we don't want to waste any. The more we grow, the more money we'll make out of them."

"That noise'd get on your nerves a bit," observed Joe.

He was right about that. The sound of all those cabbages rubbing together was nerve-rending to say the least. If you got two cabbages and rubbed them together and then magnified it a few thousand times you'd have an idea what it was like. It produced eerie shrieking noises that rippled back and forth across Arty's creeping carpet of cramped cabbages. It was especially bad in the mornings and evenings, when the temperature altered, and on a hot day it was excruciating. It could also start up for no apparent reason. It was all highly unnerving.

Because they couldn't grow outwards, the cabbages grew upwards. Some of the leaves were waist-high by this time. Cars would slow down as they passed Arty's place, experienced gardeners, baffled when it came to identifying what Arty's cabbages were. From the road it was impossible to tell because cabbages never looked like that.

Neighbours within earshot of Arty's cabbages were driven to distraction. Three of them put their homes on the market because of the noise those cabbages were making. That made it six houses for sale around Arty's place. Forlorn prospects of selling a property around there just then.

There were a number of complaints made to the police about that nerve-racking noise, and though they came and had a look and a listen there was nothing they could do about it. There's no law against growing cabbages on your own property, and you can't arrest a cabbage and charge it with disturbing the peace.

One night Carol arrived over at Joe and Helen's place in her dressing-gown with the kids in their pyjamas clutching sleeping bags. They made her a cup of tea.

"It's those ghastly cabbages," she said. "The noise is so bad tonight. I just can't stand it. It puts my nerves on edge. I don't know how Arty can sleep through it."

"Well you can just stay here until the cabbages are gone," said Helen. "I don't know how you've put up with it for this long."

"Arty reckons they'll be ready to pick in a day or two," said Joe. "I must say I'll be glad to see 'em go myself."

A few days after that Arty pronounced that the cabbages were ready for the market. They loaded boxes onto the truck and backed it up to the cabbage patch. There was no way you could get into that impenetrable wad of cabbages, so they began cutting them from one corner, and by the time they were two rows into it they discovered a remarkable thing. The cabbages were square. Square and white, with leaves sticking up like the Simpsons on telly.

"Funny-lookin' cabbages," said Joe, holding one up for Arty to have a look at.

"You know, Joe," said Arty thoughtfully, taking the cabbage off him and holding it out in one hand. "I think we might have made a breakthrough here!"

"What kind of a breakthrough?"

"Well imagine how much easier these are going to be to pack into crates, for example! Packaging is everything these days! They'll be easier to cut up for salads and things, too! Just imagine!"

"I just hope we can sell them," said Joe, cutting the top leaves off a cabbage and looking at it, square, white and crew-cut.

"Sell them?" said Arty scornfully. "Ordinary old cabbages are selling for ninety cents each at the market in Danby. And these are organically grown. Wait and see what we get for these!"

They got fifteen cents each, and only half of them sold at all. No one wanted square white cabbages with crew cuts. They weren't worth sending to the market, and they hadn't harvested enough of them to noticeably reduce the awful noise they were still making.

A local grocer took a couple of crates off them to see how they went, but he reported the same thing, people thought they looked strange, and people don't buy strange-looking things to eat. No one wanted square white cabbages with crew-cuts.

A pig farmer they knew came and took two trailer loads of them but you could hardly see where he'd taken them from. They put a sign out at the gate saying, FREE: PICK YOUR OWN CABBAGES. ORGANICALLY GROWN. NO LIMIT.

A few people stopped and looked and laughed and took a cabbage away to show their friends. The usual remark was, "I wonder what they'd be like to eat?"

After a few days Arty took the sign down again. He didn't like people's attitude towards his cabbages.

It was a Sunday. Arty, Carol, Joe and Helen were sitting in Arty and Carol's kitchen. The kids were out playing on the cabbages, they'd discovered that you could walk across the top of them and make them creak and squeak.

"There's nothing wrong with those cabbages as such," said Arty thoughtfully stirring his cup of tea. "They're perfectly good organically grown cabbages."

"But they're square," said Joe. "And people just don't want square cabbages."

"We could cut them up and sell them off to restaurants for coleslaw and salads and things," mused Arty.

"Four tons of chopped-up cabbage?" said Helen. "We might as well boil up four tons of corned beef to go with it and open a chain of restaurants."

"What do they usually do with crops they can't sell?" said Carol.

"They plough them back into the ground for fertiliser, but we couldn't do that with these," said Joe. "We haven't got enough ground. We'd end up with a hell of a mess."

"We could let Tom Johnson spray them with Roundup like he's been threatening," suggested Arty.

"He's bluffing," said Joe. "No one could afford that much Roundup."

"I know a use for them" said Carol.

"What's that?"

"We could record the sound of them and sell tapes of it to people who want to get rid of their wives or neighbours," replied Carol.

"Be serious, dear," said Arty.

"I am serious," said Carol. "Those cabbages have to go. I've told you before, it's them or me. I'm not coming home until they're all gone, and that's that."

"I agree we have to get rid of them," said Arty, "but how are we going to do it?"

"Dig a big hole and bury them?" suggested Helen.

"It'd cost too much to dig a hole big enough to take them," said Arty.

"What's to stop us loading them onto the truck and taking them to the tip?" said Joe.

"No," said Arty. "We're not putting them in the tip."

"Why not?"

"It's too embarrassing," said Arty. "People'd laugh at us."

"Laugh?" said Carol. "What do you think they're doing now? We're already the laughing-stock of the whole district!"

Arty finally agreed that the cabbages would have to be carted away and dumped. They put the sides on his old truck and loaded them on with a borrowed front-end loader. Then they took them up the river and down a side road and tipped them into a small scrubby creek that ran into Boulder Creek. Five full loads of them.

Finally all that was left of Arty's cabbages was a scattering of leaves and a churned-up patch of bare ground behind the shed. None of them had had a single feed of those cabbages. It must have been the unappetising noise they made, plus the fact that people don't like square white cabbages with crew cuts.

But they still hadn't seen the last of those cabbages of Arty's. A couple of weeks after they'd dumped them there were four days and nights of heavy rain. The Turnbull River came up twenty feet, and at the height of the flood big rafts of cabbages began floating down past Matea, and as the flood subsided every backwater and shingle bar and river beach was covered with rotting square cabbages. Arty and Joe received an invitation to call round to the police station, right now.

The sergeant was looking grim.

"Did you blokes dump all those cabbages of yours in the river?" he said.

"No, Sarge," said Arty. "We dumped them in a gully up near Boulder Creek. The flood must have washed them into the river."

"Why didn't you just bury them, or put them in the dump?"

"People were laughing at us, Sarge," said Arty. "We were too embarrassed to put them in the tip."

"You know it's an offence to illegally dump organic refuse," said the sergeant. "You could be fined up to a thousand dollars for that."

"Aw, come on, Sarge. Give us a break. We had a bad run of luck with those cabbages. They've already cost us a packet."

"That's no excuse for scattering the bloody things all over the place," said the sergeant. "They're even getting sucked into the irrigation pumps down at Knowles and blocking the intakes. There's rotten bloody cabbages all the way down the bloody river! Who do you think's going to clean it all up?"

"They'll rot away in no time," said Arty.

"Well you'll rot away if you pull another stunt like that," said the sergeant. "You'll rot away in jail. Now get the hell out of here before I book you!"

"I don't think I'll bother with market gardening any more," said Arty as they drove away from the police station in Joe's ute. "There's too much risk involved."

PAT TROMBETH

THE FOX

AROUND THIS time an unfortunate thing was happening in Matea. The whole town had a stroke of very bad luck. After nearly ten years of letting just about everybody off just about everything, the Matea traffic cop retired and a new one was due to take up duty there. It was a wet day and they were sitting in Arty and Carol's kitchen with cups of tea and biscuits.

"This new traffic cop that's coming is supposed to be a bit hard," said Arty, dunking a biscuit in his tea. "Cliff James has heard about him."

Cliff James was the Matea Community Constable and well-liked by everyone.

"What does Cliff reckon?" asked Joe.

"He's a bloke called Fox," said Arty. "They reckon he's particularly tough on drinking drivers.""Well we weren't going to get another traffic cop like old Vince," said Joe.

"I'm going to miss him," said Arty. "We'll just have to wait and see how this new traffic cop turns out."

The new traffic cop turned out to be a thorough-going ratbag. His name was Tom Fox but very soon everyone was calling him Foxy, because that's what he was, foxy. He lurked and prowled and hid in ambush, and stalked even old Sarah Harding the librarian and gave her a ticket for an expired Warrant of Fitness and a bald tyre.

He'd check the pub carpark out to see who was in there and then wait round the corner and pull them up and breath-test them when they left. Nine of them lost their drivers' licences in the first six weeks of Foxy. He was highly unpopular. He lived alone. He was short and stooped and foxy-looking. He had a limp. He never smiled. He darkened the atmosphere of Matea (pop. 1675). Behind his back he became known as 'The Fox'.

The first run-in Arty and Joe had with The Fox happened when Matea was getting ready for Christmas. Every year Arty used to let the younger kids at the school decorate his old truck for the Matea Christmas Float Parade. This year they turned it into a big boat with painted cardboard, and a bunch of them were done up like little Vikings. Even Arty and Joe in the cab had false beards and cardboard Viking hats on. But on the way to join the parade Foxy pulled them over and inspected the truck and wrote out a ticket for Arty for no Registration, no Certificate of Fitness, two dangerously-worn tyres and driving an unsafe vehicle.

"I can't let you drive on the road with these children with a vehicle in this condition," said Foxy, handing the ticket to Arty.

"But we've been doing this every year for years," said Arty.

"Well you're not doing it this year," said Foxy. "Your steering's sloppy, your brakes are spongy, your tyres are dangerously worn, you've no headlights or indicators or horn working, no windscreen wipers – this whole vehicle is in an unsafe condition."

"But we're only doing ten Ks an hour on a fine day," protested Arty.

"If you drive it anywhere but directly from here to your place I'll put a dangerous driving charge on you," said Foxy.

A great cry of dismay went up from the kids on the float, but Foxy was impervious to it. He got into his car and drove off and parked up on the corner, watching them.

"Sorry, kids," said Arty, taking his hat and beard off. "You heard him, we can't go in the parade."

You can imagine how popular Foxy was over that. If he'd been a fly instead of a fox those kids would have cheerfully pulled all his legs and wings off. He followed them all the way to Arty's place and they had to make three trips in the ute to get all the kids to the parade at all.

If Foxy ever had any popularity in Matea he lost a fair bit of it when it got round about him stopping the kids going in the Christmas parade, but his popularity with his victims wasn't a concern of Foxy's. His tyres were let down when he was at the school lecturing the kids about road safety, but that only fuelled Foxy's fanatical professional fastidiousness. He began handing out warning notices to kids riding bikes on footpaths.

Arty and Joe were both out of work again. They were leaning on the bar in the pub, wondering what to do.

"No one's got the rubbish-collection contract yet," said Joe. "The bloke who was doing it has moved over to Knowles, driving a digger on the stop-banks. The Council's been doing it themselves for the last few weeks."

"We might be able to get Bob Bremner to put in a word for us," said Arty. "We could get my truck done up and use that, if we get the job."

Bob Bremner was the County Engineer. Arty and Joe had both worked for him from time to time. He was a good bloke.

"Let's give it a go!" said Joe.

Carol and Helen approached the idea with a certain amount of caution, trying to imagine how Arty and Joe could come undone running a rubbish collection. They finally agreed, and Arty and Joe bailed Bob Bremner up in his office and asked him to put in a word with the Borough Council for them.

"I can't tell the Council who to give contracts to," said Bob.

"You're on the Council yourself, aren't you?" said Arty.

"Yes, but I haven't got anything to do with letting contracts. That's the Maintenance Committee."

"Yes but you know them, don't you? You could stick in a word for us, couldn't you?"

"I can't go sticking in words for people," said Bob. "It doesn't work that way. I suppose I could give you a reference to put in with your application. That's about all I can do for you, I'm afraid."

"There's actually another thing you could help us out with, Bob," said Arty.

"What's that?" said Bob guardedly.

"We need to know what it's costing the Council to run the rubbish collection so we can put in a competitive price."

"Absolutely out of the question!" said Bob. "I can't go handing out information like that!"

"There's nothing wrong with rate-payers knowing what their rubbish collection costs, is there?"

"That information's available in the Annual Report."

"We can't wait for that," said Arty. "We need to know now. Come on, Bob. We've always done good work for you, haven't we?"

"Well, I could mention your interest to Norman Frazer this afternoon," said Bob, anxious to get them out of his office. "I'm meeting with him this afternoon on another matter. I'm not promising anything, but if it comes up I'll see what I can do for you."

"Thanks, Bob, you're a trooper! We'll give you a ring in the morning, eh?"

"Yes, all right. I might have something for you by then. Now if you'll excuse me, I've got a meeting in a few minutes."

And the next day they found out that the Council was spending over a thousand dollars a week on rubbish collection and would look favourably on an application for a private contract. All that without Bob actually saying it straight-out. They filed an application with the Town Clerk, then they took Arty's old truck down to the garage to find out what it was going to cost to get a Certificate of Fitness for it. Six hundred and fifty dollars, at least, and that's if they did a lot of the minor work themselves.

Fortunately Arty had some tyres with a bit of tread left on them in his yard, and a horn that worked in his shed, and he and Joe were both handy with a spanner. They had thirty days to pay off the garage.

They had to apply to Foxy for a Commercial Operator's Licence, and he went over the truck and sent them away three times for minor things, and then mucked them around for three weeks before giving them one. By this time they had a contract with the Council to do the twice-weekly Matea rubbish collection. They knocked up some high wooden sides for Arty's truck, which now even had brakes and lights and a new battery.

The first collection went off without a hitch. They took it in turns to throw the rubbish bags onto the truck. It was hard work but it only took three and a half hours to do the whole town.

"Eight hundred and fifty bucks a week for seven hours' work!" said Arty. "Not bad, eh!"

They'd been doing the rubbish for less than a month when the first incident happened. They'd scored a job on the side, disposing of reject apples from the Matea Orchards. They'd loaded two and a half tons of apples onto the truck and were driving back through town to get to the tip. Arty was driving, and he must have knocked the hoist into gear, and as they drove up the road the tray of the truck rose up in the air, and just as they noticed the truck handling strangely the tailboard tripped and there was a great rush as two and a half tons of reject apples poured out onto the road, which was completely blocked. A deluge of apples, spilling out across the footpaths on both sides, right on a bend.

Joe ran to stop the traffic and Arty dropped the hoist and drove to the Council Depot to get a front-end loader to come and load the apples back onto the truck. The traffic was held up for half an hour while they cleared a lane through the apples.

Foxy didn't help much by turning up and demanding to know how it happened and making it sound as serious as possible. It was almost dark by the time they'd swept up the last of the apples and shovelled them onto the truck. Foxy wrote them out a Traffic Offence Notice for casting dangerous litter on the road and obstructing traffic.

"You lot are the worst menace on the roads around here," he said, handing Arty the ticket. "First it was cabbages and now it's apples."

"No, Foxy," said Arty, screwing up the ticket and dropping it onto the ground. "You're the worst menace we've ever had on the roads around here!"

Foxy almost smiled. He liked getting people rattled.

Less than a week after that the other rubbish-collecting incident happened, the last. They'd collected a full load of rubbish and were heading for the tip with it. Someone must have put some live ashes in their paper rubbish-bag and the wind fanned it into a blaze. By the time they noticed anything half the load was alight.

"Bloody hell!" shouted Arty, looking through the rear window. "The load's on fire!"

"What are we going to do?" said Joe.

"Go like hell for the dump. We might be able to ditch it before it sets the truck on fire!"

But they didn't have a chance. There was about a mile to go to the tip and the faster they went the more the fire got fanned. Before they'd got halfway there the wooden sides of the truck were alight. Someone in a car behind them was blowing their horn continuously.

"The truck's on fire now," said Arty. "We're not going to make it. Pull up, Joe. We'd better bail out in case the petrol tank goes up underneath us."

Joe stopped the truck in the middle of the road and they scrambled out and stood back from it. The whole rear end of the vehicle was ablaze and the paint on the cab was starting to blacken and blister. The heat was savage, they had to move further away from it.

A crowd began to gather. The hydraulic-oil reservoir went up with a roar, and suddenly the inside of the cab was a whirling blaze. A great grey-black column of smoke was billowing up into the sky. The petrol tank exploded in a whooshing fireball.

Someone must have called the Fire Service, they could hear the siren, but by the time the appliance got there the tyres on the rubbish truck were blazing. She was a write-off. By the time they'd got the fire out all that was left of the truck was a twisted blackened skeleton, surrounded by burnt cans and bottles and lumps of sodden, steaming, stinking rubbish. It was a desolate scene.

Foxy had arrived and was redirecting the traffic, his prowl-car parked in the roadway with its red light flashing. When he had the traffic sorted out he came limping over to where Arty and Joe were standing.

"Well, well, well," said Foxy. "And how did this happen?"

"Our bloody load went on fire," said Arty. "I suppose there's a law against that, is there?"

"Who are you insured with? This vehicle becomes their property now."

"Can't tell you off-hand," said Arty. "We'll have to let you know."

"Well the wreck will be stored in the Council yards until the insurance assessors decide what they want to do with it. You might as well go home. I'll organise the cleaning-up."

Cliff James gave them a lift to Arty's place in a police car. On the way they passed a Council truck and front-end loader, on their way to clean up the mess. They had a cup of tea. Carol arrived home with the kids. They'd already heard about the fire, the whole school had. By now the whole of Matea had.

"Well that's that," said Arty. "And no bloody insurance."

"Wasn't the truck insured?" said Carol.

"Never got round to it," shrugged Arty.

"That means we've lost the truck?"

Arty nodded.

"Plus what it's going to cost to clean up the mess," said Joe.

"What do we do now?" said Helen.

"We can't collect the rubbish without a truck," said Arty. "Unless one drops out of the sky we're going to lose the contract. We'll have to let them know we can't go on doing it. They'll probably take it over themselves again. I'll give them a ring."

He was right. Three days later they were formally advised that their rubbish-collection contract was terminated. The Council had resumed doing it themselves. The enclosed first and final cheque was just enough to cover the cost of getting the truck done up and disposing of its remains.

"What's our next move?" said Joe, throwing the contract-terminating letter onto the table.

"How much money have we got left?" said Arty.

"None," said Helen.

"That's a coincidence," said Arty.

"Huh?" said Joe.

"It's almost exactly what Hugh Gardiner wants for someone to take over his tree-felling business for a while."

"Oh no!" said Carol. "Not another crazy scheme!"

"No, dear," said Arty. "It's a good deal. I was talking to Hugh yesterday. He's got a contract worth forty thousand dollars. He can't do it himself and he's going to lose it if it doesn't get started on."

"Why doesn't he do it himself?" said Helen.

"Hugh can't get around much any more. He had an accident."

"What happened to him?" asked Joe.

"Fell out of a tree and fractured his hip and it won't come right. The poor beggar can hardly walk."

"It sounds dangerous to me," said Carol.

"It doesn't need to be dangerous," said Joe. "I've done heaps of tree felling. What's the contract, Arty?"

"A row of pines out on McLeod Road has to come out. They're widening the road there. We can have any timber that's in it, the rest of it has to be burned or dumped. Hugh reckons it's about a month's work. He's prepared to supply all the gear and go halves."

"Twenty thousand dollars for a month's work sounds all right to me," said Joe.

"I'll ring Hugh and see if we can get the job, eh?" said Arty.

"Sure," said Joe.

"I don't mind," said Helen after a pause.

They looked at Carol, who was still looking sceptical.

"All right, if you must," she said. "But I still don't like the sound of it."

"I'll ring Hugh," said Arty. "He should be back from the Medical Centre by now. He's been having treatment."

The assets of the tree-felling business turned out to be an old four-wheel-drive tractor with a bucket and blade on it, two chainsaws, one of them nearly new, a collection of ropes and wedges and some axes and mauls and two tree-felling signs.

"It's all we need," said Joe. "With this tractor we can hook a rope onto a tree and drag it in any direction we like."

The following day Arty and Joe went out to McLeod Road to inspect the job. It was a 150-yard row of fairly old pine trees, about twenty feet back from the edge of the road and closely planted. The trees had been planted close to a fence and had grown around it. There was wire through every trunk to a height of three-feet-six. Then they found that the ground on the other side of the trees was very swampy.

"We can't work the tractor in that," said Joe. "You'd be bellied before you went ten yards."

"But there's some good timber in there," said Arty. "If we cut them off above the old fence and drop them across the road we can cut the heads off and shove them to that side with the tractor and push the logs to this side."

"We'd have to hold up the traffic," said Joe.

"We know how to do that," said Arty. "We've got those signs."

"What about The Fox?" said Joe.

"We can't go worrying about Foxy all the time," said Arty. "He doesn't come out here anyway, there's hardly any traffic on this road. Nothing's come past all the time we've been here. We'll get away with it."

The next day they went out there with the ute and tractor and got started. They set up the signs and Arty got ready to stop any traffic that came along.

Joe felled a tree straight across the road. Arty trimmed the branches off it and topped it and Joe on the tractor shoved the branches and heads to one side of the road and the log to the other. It worked fine. One stock-truck and two cars came along and they only held them up for a few minutes. No one minded.

By lunch time they'd felled eight trees. The road was in a bit of a mess and the pile of branches and heads was a bit overwhelming. A tangle of broken branches and foliage shoved up as high as a house.

"It'll settle down to less than half that," said Arty. "Then we'll burn it."

"I wonder what those logs are worth?" said Joe.

"We'll stop off at the mill on the way home and get someone to come out and have a look at them," said Arty.

They made good progress over the next few days and had felled about a third of the row of trees when they had an unfortunate accident, involving The Fox. Arty and Joe were felling a tree when Foxy bowled up the road in his prowl car and drove straight past their sign and pulled up and got out of the car, brandishing his ticket-book. Arty saw him just in time.

"Look out!" he shouted.

The tree cracked. Joe stopped the chainsaw and stood back. Foxy looked up at the toppling tree and ran for it. The tree fell with a crash. It fell right across Foxy's patrol car. The roof was squashed into the seats and the chassis was almost touching the ground. They stared unbelieving at it. It was suddenly so quiet you could hear Foxy's stomach gurgling.

"You lot have done it good and properly this time," said Foxy. "Look what you've done to my car!"

"You parked it there," said Arty. "Didn't you see our sign?"

He stared at the flattened patrol car, trying to keep a straight face.

"I'll sign you!" snarled Foxy. "What's the idea of cutting trees down across a public road like this?"

"They have to come down," said Arty. "They're widening the road here."

"Who authorised this?" demanded Foxy.

"It's a government job," said Arty. "They're not going to give out contracts that aren't authorised, are they?"

"Get this tree off my car and clear up this mess. I'm ordering you to stop cutting down these trees until the matter's been thoroughly investigated. There'll be some serious charges laid over this, I promise you!"

They cut through the trunk of the tree on either side of Foxy's car and shoved the log off it with the bucket of the tractor, popping the only unbroken window in the process, the rear one.

"Careful, Joe," called out Arty. "Don't damage that car!"

Joe bladed the branches and logs off the road. Arty loaded their gear onto the ute. Foxy stood and watched for traffic. There was none. Finally all that was left in the roadway was Foxy's squashed car. It was a pathetic sight.

"Are you going to leave that there?" asked Joe, idling the tractor.

"Do you think I'm going to drive it away?" said Foxy sarcastically, going over to the car and pulling at the driver's door. It was buckled and jammed shut. He reached in through the broken window and found his radio handpiece and tried it. It was dead.

"I'll shove it off the road for you if you like," said Joe. "It's a bit dangerous parked there like that."

"All right then, move it off the road," snapped Foxy.

Joe put his bucket under the side of the broken-backed prowl car and began to push it to the side of the road, but the far side of it jammed into the road and the car began to tip over, so Joe kept pushing until it rolled right over onto its roof. By this time it was off the road with its wheels in the air.

"Did you have to do that?" shouted Foxy. "You've done even more damage now!"

"I reckon she's a write-off all right," said Arty seriously, shaking his head from side to side. "I hope you're insured!"

"You'll pay for this!" said Foxy.

He groped into the window of the upturned car and retrieved a torch and a book and a couple of other things. Arty had found his ticket book lying among some branches and had it stuffed into his pocket to be disposed of later.

"We'll give you a ride into town if you like, Foxy," said Arty generously.

Foxy hesitated.

"There's not much traffic out here," said Arty. "You'd better hop in."

Foxy climbed into the ute. It was a bit of a squeeze. He sat hunched and silent against the door all the way into town. They let him off at the police station. He got out and slammed the door and limped off without a word. Arty and Joe drove off and a few yards up the road they burst into laughter.

"I don't care what he does to us," gasped Arty. "It was worth it to see that tree land on that car of his!"

In due course they received a summons charging them with wilful damage to a police car, obstructing a public road in such a manner as to cause danger to the public, and illegal use of traffic signs. They stood and faced the Magistrate.

"This isn't the first time you two have been before me on charges relating to your casual attitude towards the regulations," said the Magistrate. "I'm fining you a thousand dollars on the dangerous obstruction charge, and I invite the county engineers to consider your fitness to carry out this kind of work. On the charge of illegal use of traffic signs you are convicted and discharged . . . Mr Fox."

"Your Honour," said Foxy, standing up.

"You say these people felled a tree on your patrol car?"

"Yes, Your Honour."

"Didn't you receive some kind of warning that tree-felling was in progress there?"

"No, Your Honour," lied Foxy.

"What was on these illegally-placed road signs?"

"Stop. Tree-felling in progress, Your Honour, but they were . . ."

"And you drove past that sign, ignored it?"

"Yes, Your Honour. I thought . . ."

"And a tree fell on your car?"

"Yes, Your Honour. They . . ."

"I'm dismissing the charge of wilful damage to a police vehicle," said the magistrate. "And I find that negligence on the part of Officer Fox contributed in no small way to this incident. Call the next case."

They retreated to Arty and Carol's place.

"A thousand dollars!" said Arty. "We haven't got away with much at that price!"

"We can kiss that contract goodbye too, by the sound of it," said Joe.

"Where does that leave us?" said Carol.

"Right back where you started," said Helen. "No money and no work."

"Something'll crop up," said Arty philosophically.

"I wonder what it's going to be?" said Joe.

"So do I," sighed Carol.

The county engineers took the magistrate's advice and reconsidered Arty and Joe's fitness to carry out their tree-felling work. They decided to terminate the contract. They were awarded $6,000 as a progress payment, from which $3,000 was deducted for clearing up the mess they'd left behind them. By the time they'd given Hugh Gardiner his half and paid the fine and their expenses, they were back where they'd started. Broke and out of work, just as Helen said.

DANGER
1080
POISON
LAID HER
JEYES FLUID
PAT TREMBETH

With a Hiss and a Roar

"YOU'VE GONE through two jobs and two thousand dollars in less than two months!" said Carol. "And you're lucky not to have ended up in jail. So much for your crazy schemes. Why can't you get ordinary work, like ordinary people?"

"What's more ordinary than collecting rubbish or felling trees?" said Arty. "No, we've just had a bad run of luck, that's all, dear. We'll come right. Something'll crop up."

"That's what I'm afraid of," sighed Carol.

In the next month they got three small jobs. The first was repainting Matea's two pedestrian crossings. That went off without a hitch. Then they sand-blasted off a big black crack some kids had painted across the road outside the school when they were supposed to be painting the school gates.

One of Arty's kids was involved in that escapade and Carol got more agitated about it than the occasion called for. She was always very sensitive to any signs of the boy turning out like his old man. He'd already been described by one teacher as a 'Holy Little Terror'.

Their third job did have a hitch, quite a bad one. They hadn't worked for nearly a week. One evening Arty rang Joe.

"I've got us a job," he said. "It'll only take us a day, but it's worth fifty bucks. I've told them we'll do it."

"What is it?" said Joe.

"We've got to dig a new hole for the long-drop behind the pub and shift the lavatory over it. The old one's full."

The pub had three two-bed units in the backyard where the larrikins from the bush stayed when they were in town, and the outside lavatory was for these units. The pub itself operated along more modern lines.

Arty and Joe turned up at the pub with some tools on the ute and went into the bar. The publican poured them a beer and explained what he wanted.

"All you have to do is dig us a new hole and shift the lavatory onto it and cover over the old hole," he said. "I've got to go over to Danby on business, I'll pay you when I get back this afternoon."

"Not a problem, Jack," said Arty. "We'll handle that for you."

Jack left for Danby and Arty and Joe had another beer while they were there, and discussed how they were going to approach the job. They gave Bulge the barman a chit for the cost of the beers, to be deducted from the fifty dollars Jack was going to owe them. An old coal-miner called Mick Haines wandered in and joined them, so they had another beer with him.

"What have you blokes been up to?" said Mick.

"Nothin' much," said Arty. "We're diggin' a new hole for Jack's long-drop today."

"What are you doing that for?" said Mick, putting his glass loudly on the bar. "Thanks Bulge."

"Because the old one's full," said Arty. "We're going to dig a new hole and shift the building across onto it."

"Na," said Mick scornfully, quaffing deeply from his fresh beer. "That's not the way to go about it."

"How do you go about it then?" said Joe.

"It's dead easy," said Mick. "You stick half a plug of

Molanite in the bottom of the hole and blow a nest. It drains the hole and she's all brand-new again."

Arty and Joe looked at each other. They knew that miners were expert at handling explosives.

"That sounds more like it!" said Arty. "Have one on us, Mick."

After some further consultation Joe hopped in the ute and shot down to the County Depot to get some Molanite, while Mick and Arty worked out the finer details of the undertaking. Joe came back with two plugs of explosive, two detonators and two feet of fuse.

"I told them we were blowing a stump," said Joe. "I had to take enough explosive to make it look right."

They took the Molanite out to the job. Mick crimped a foot of fuse into a detonator and poked the detonator into a full plug of Molanite.

"Might as well make a decent job of it for them," he said.

They solved the problem of getting the charge into the bottom of the hole. They tied the plug to the forked end of the prop from the clothes-line in the pub yard. It was about ten feet long.

"Now we've got to be a bit careful here," said Mick. "I ran into a bit of trouble doin' this once."

"Yeah?" said Arty.

"Yeah?" said Joe.

"Yeah," said Mick. "We got our charge set and lit it, but when we tried to get our pole down the hole it wouldn't go. It jammed against the top of the doorway with the charge barely below ground level."

"Hell!" said Joe.

"What happened?" said Arty.

"We had to leave it there and take off, and when she

went up it blew the thing to bits. Sheets of iron flyin' in all directions!"

"We don't want that happening here," said Arty.

"It's not goin' to," said Mick. "I'm gunna make good and sure before I light the fuse this time!"

They tried the angle of the pole down through the doorway. It was marginal, they couldn't tell for sure without immersing the charge, and they didn't want to do that before it was lit.

"We don't want anything to go wrong," said Arty. "We'd better knock the roof off. We can stick it back on when the job's done. Won't take a minute."

They took the four short sheets of corrugated iron off the roof of the lavatory, fed the pole up through the roof, lit the fuse, and plunged the pole down into the hole. It didn't reach the bottom but by this time they were in no position to do anything about that. They got round the corner of the pub, about fifty feet away, and waited for the explosion.

There was a muffled crack.

"Sounds like the detonator's pulled out of the plug on the way down," said Mick. "But we'd better leave it for a while to make sure it's not a piece of hang-fire fuse."

So they retired to the bar and got Bulge to reactivate their chit.

"What do we do now?" said Joe.

"We'll have to pull it up again and put another charge down," said Mick professionally.

So they had another beer and went back out to the yard. With the help of some sacks they extracted the disgusting clothes-prop, whereupon they found that the plug of Molanite had come off somewhere down there. It had been tied on to be pushed, but not pulled.

"Just as well we did get a bit of extra Molanite," said

Mick. "We'll make good and sure this time."

He prepared another charge and this time he taped the detonator and fuse firmly onto the plug. Then he lit the fuse and they returned it to the depths and got back around the corner.

"I hope that plug doesn't set the other one off," said Mick.

And just then it did. There was a startling WOOMPH! that shook the ground, and at the same time a spectacular thing happened. A great spume of stuff geysered up through the open roof of the lavatory, shading out the sun for a moment, and then it fell in a putrid, maggoty, papery shower over the whole area.

There was a stunned, ear-ringing silence.

"Bloody hell!" said Joe. "I think we've used too much explosive!"

"It wasn't supposed to do that!" said Mick.

"I think we might have mucked up again," said Arty, looking around at the mess.

Three or four people came running out of the pub.

"What was that bang?" said Bulge.

"It's all right," said Arty. "We just let off a small charge."

Thus reassured, Bulge and his clientele were only too happy to retreat back inside, away from the nauseating smell that pervaded the atmosphere.

"What do we do now?" said Joe.

"Start cleanin' up, I suppose," said Arty.

"I've just got to pop down to the Medical Centre to pick up me pills," said Mick, sidling away towards the street. "I might catch up with you blokes later. We've cleaned out the hole for them anyway."

"Okay, Mick," said Arty. "Thanks for your help."

"You're welcome, don't mention it." And he was gone.

"He could have at least stayed and helped us clean up," muttered Joe. "It's his bloody fault, all this."

"Yeah, but it's our responsibility," said Arty. "Let's get as much of it cleaned up as we can before Jack gets back from Danby. He's not going to be too chuffed about this lot."

It was inevitable that someone would report the explosion to the police, if they hadn't heard it themselves. Arty and Joe had just started hosing down the pub roof when Sergeant Freeman and Cliff James turned up.

"What was that explosion, Arty?" said the sergeant.

"Nothin' much, Sarge," said Arty. "We were just opening up the long-drop hole."

"Look at this bloody mess you've made! Whew!"

"Yeah, sorry about that, Sarge. She blew back on us."

"I'm going to have to charge you with this, Arty," said the sergeant. "You'd better come down to the station and give us a statement. Cliff – you'd better get hold of the Fire Service to come and hose down this mess. And you'd better call up Foxy on the radio and get him down here."

The only consolation for Arty and Joe was as they drove off behind the police car, they saw The Fox standing in the intersection outside the pub with a handkerchief over his nose and mouth, retching and gagging as he directed the traffic away from the fetid pollution that festooned everything in the vicinity.

"Weak stomach!" grinned Arty.

You could smell it up at the police station. In fact, in the entire history of Matea, nothing like that awful smell had ever been inflicted upon its citizens. Within half an hour of the explosion the tearooms, the butcher shop, the grocery store, the chemist shop, and of course the pub, were all closed up and the staff gone home. Within an hour nearly every shop in the town was closed. Several people claimed it made them sick and were treated and discharged from the Medical Centre. They had to let the kids go home from school early. All traffic was diverted away from the main street, which was deserted.

Firemen with breathing apparatus hosed down the buildings and streets as best they could, but they couldn't do anything about the smell.

Pockets of that terrible smell hung around the town for days. A whiff of it could pop up anywhere. It was particularly bad around the pub and down the main street, which must have been very bad for business. Some of the more squeamish had to leave town for a spell, and one family they heard of packed up and moved away altogether. Some people claimed they could still smell it two weeks later, but that was probably nothing but plain paranoia.

No one, not one person in Matea, sided with Arty and Joe over that smell they'd made. In fact their unpopularity eclipsed that of Foxy himself while it lasted.

Arty always said that it wouldn't have been anywhere near as bad if a decent wind had been blowing at the time. The police were unimpressed and refused to accept this rather weak defence. They went ahead and pressed charges.

The Fox didn't need to be at the court case, but he was there, like a fox at the edge of a feast.

"Using explosives in a built-up area, using explosives without a Quarryman's Licence, and casting offensive matter," said the Magistrate to Arty and Joe. "You two are becoming something of a danger to the community. Have you got anything to say in response to these charges?"

"Well, sir," said Arty. "It was actually an accident. The first plug pulled off our pole, and the second one set the first one off as well. It wouldn't have happened otherwise."

"I don't accept that it was an accident," said the

Magistrate. "Your behaviour was dangerously irresponsible, to say the least. You're lucky that no one was injured, or worse. If you keep coming before me on these sort of charges I'm going to have to consider imposing prison sentences on you. On the charge of using explosives in a built-up area I'm fining you each five hundred dollars. On the charge of using explosives without a Quarryman's Licence I'm fining you two hundred and fifty dollars each. On the charge of casting offensive matter you're each fined one hundred dollars, the fines to be paid within fourteen days or three months' imprisonment. You can stand down."

"Hell!" said Joe when they were back out on the street. "How much is that he fined us?"

"Seventeen hundred dollars," said Arty. "And we didn't even get paid for cleaning out Jack's long-drop. Some jobs just aren't worth doin'."

"You can say that again," said Joe. "How are we going to pay seventeen hundred dollars within two weeks?"

"We'll have to borrow it off Helen and Carol," said Arty. "There's no other way we can rake up the money."

"I don't know," said Carol, giving a big sigh and rolling her eyes heavenward. "You two can't even dig a hole without getting into trouble!"

ENQUIRE ABOUT
ROAD CONDITIONS
AT HOTEL

INNKEEPERS

THEY HAD to use every source of money they had access to, including borrowing from friends, but they got the fines paid in time. Arty and Joe were now in debt to their wives and others, but they were still keen to do something about it. They carried on doing casual and part-time work, waiting for the big one to turn up.

There was one minor hitch when they were doing a painting job at the Matea Hospital. A container of paint–thinner got spilt and the fumes got sucked into the hospital's air-conditioning and a whole ward had to be evacuated. They had to make a statement to the police about it, but no actual charges were laid.

Then there was the pub. Arty's cousin Merv had the Turnbull Tavern at the junction of the Western Highway and the Turnbull Pass road, a small roadside pub forty Ks out of Matea. Unless the pass was blocked by snow or slips there wasn't much reason for anyone to stop there, but they made a living. Arty and Joe usually stopped there for a drink and a yarn when they were out that way.

Arty's cousin's wife was an Aussie and her grandfather had died. They were flying over for the funeral and to see her family, and Merv put it on Arty and Joe to run the pub for them while they were away.

"Not a problem, Merv," said Arty. "I've run bars before."

They spent half a day out there, learning the ropes, and then they were on their own, leaning on the bar, watching for traffic. There wasn't much of it and no one even slowed down at the Turnbull Tavern.

"It's a bit quiet," said Joe.

"Yeah," said Arty. "I reckon this pub's too close to Matea to do much good. If they're going to Matea they're nearly there, and if they're going to the coast they've only just left. And no one'd be game to come out here for a few beers with Foxy around."

"They must stop here sometimes," said Joe. "Merv seems to make a living out of it."

"He wouldn't make much out of it at this rate," said Arty. "We haven't sold a beer all day."

Around four o'clock a car stopped and a woman came in to ask if the pass was open. A bit later two musterers stopped in for a beer. One beer, and then they bought a tray of cans and took off for the coast. A couple with three kids stopped to use the toilet around five o'clock, and just after that a commercial traveller came in and skulled three double whiskies and half a pint of Speights and shot through.

Arty and Joe ate bread and cheese and stoked up the open fire in the bar and waited for the evening rush. It didn't happen.

"Not exactly what you'd call a roaring trade," said Arty around ten o'clock. "We've taken less than thirty bucks all day."

"It might pick up tomorrow," said Joe.

"I sure hope so," said Arty.

At eleven o'clock they closed the bar, heated and ate some baked beans, and went to bed in the living quarters at the back of the pub. They'd decided to stay there at night while Merv was away because of security reasons.

The next morning they ate, cleaned up the bar, lit the fire, opened the pub, and waited. There was some traffic but none stopped. Around half-past eleven a bloke pulled in but he only wanted a packet of smokes.

"This is ridiculous," said Arty. "We need a way to attract a bit of business. I'll go nuts if it keeps on like this."

"They wouldn't stop if you offered them free beer," said Joe, watching a truck roar past.

"Just a minute!" said Arty. "That's not a silly idea! What if we offered them the first beer on the house? That ought to pull them in."

"Couldn't do any harm to try it," said Joe.

"We'll put up a sign," said Arty.

"I don't know," said Joe dubiously. "The last time we put a sign up it didn't work out too good."

"That was cabbages," said Arty. "This is beer. Everyone wants beer, especially free beer."

They found a tin of white paint out in the shed and painted their sign on a sheet of hardboard and nailed it to the signpost on the corner. It said FREE BEER TODAY.

"That should do the trick," said Arty, standing back to look at the sign. "Now we'll just go in and wait for them."

They didn't have long to wait. A car pulled up and three big young blokes came into the bar.

"Free beer, eh?" said one of them.

"Yep," said Arty, pouring three beers. "The first one's on the house."

"It doesn't say anything about the first one on your sign, it just says free beer."

"Yeah, but it only means the first one's free."

"That a fact?"

They took their beers over to one of the tables and talked for a while and drank the beer, came and put the empty glasses on the bar and left the pub.

A couple of minutes later they came back in.

"I'll have another first one, thanks barman," said one of them.

"Me too," said another.

"What the hell," muttered Arty. "Give them another beer, Joe."

An hour later they were still there, going out and coming in again and hooking into the free beer and getting boisterous. Arty and Joe didn't quite know how to handle the situation. By this time they'd been joined by two couples on holiday in a camper-van, and they were enjoying free beer as well.

"You'd better go out and rip that bloody sign down, Joe," said Arty. "We can't go on giving free beer away like this."

Joe stuck the sign round the back of the pub but it was too late. The activity in the pub seemed to attract more customers, and everyone who came in was immediately advised by the other customers that the beer was free today. Arty and Joe put on another keg and wished everyone would go away. They were out of their depth. If they stopped serving this lot they'd start helping themselves.

By dark that night there was a roaring party going on in the Turnbull Tavern. There were about forty people jammed into the little bar. One of the original blokes was getting stroppy and suddenly a fight broke out between him and a possum-trapper. It quickly developed into a brawl that spilled out into the road. A thrown jug smashed two bottles of spirits and a woman started screaming. The back-log rolled out of the fire and lay burning on the carpet, filling the bar with acrid smoke. And in the middle of all this Foxy limped into the bar.

"What's going on here?" he shouted above the racket.

"What does it look like?" said Arty, fending off a woman who'd been pushed into him. "They just started fighting."

"What are you two doing here?"

"We're running the pub. It belongs to my cousin."

"You call this running a pub? You know you're not supposed to serve liquor to people who've already had too much to drink. I'll be reporting this!"

"Why don't you do something about stopping it?" said Arty, as the front window of the pub shattered beside them and a half-full bottle of beer just missed Foxy's head.

Foxy went outside. His uniform was having its effect. The shouting and swearing faded. Vehicles were taking off. The bar emptied and Arty slammed the door and locked it. More cars departed, and then all was quiet. They heard later that Foxy chased after the three louts who'd started it all and breath-tested the driver and booked him for excess alcohol.

Arty and Joe stood among the smoky wreckage of the

bar. There was broken glass all over the place, beer spilt everywhere, a big patch of burnt carpet, a black high-heeled shoe lying on the floor by the dart board.

"I wonder how much beer we went through?" said Joe.

"We're well into the third keg," said Arty. "We'll have to try and make it up somehow. In the meantime we'd better start cleaning up this mess."

It was after midnight by the time they'd cleaned up all the broken glass and spilt beer and restored the bar to some kind of order. They put a mat from the lounge over the burnt patch of carpet, and nailed their FREE BEER TODAY sign over the broken front window, with the words facing inwards. Then they ate and went to bed.

The next day they were leaning on the bar watching the glazier from Matea fitting new glass in the front window, and waiting for customers.

"Three kegs of beer," said Arty. "That's going to take a bit of accounting for."

"We'll just have to pay for it ourselves," said Joe.

"It'd be better if we could trade our way out of it somehow, said Arty. "If only we could find some way to get people to stop here."

"We could stop all the Turnbull Pass traffic if there was a slip or a heavy fall of snow up there," said Joe.

"What's to stop us putting the barrier across and telling them there's a temporary hold-up on the pass?" said Arty. "They could have a beer or two while they're waiting and then we can let them go again."

"We could try it, I suppose," said Joe. "Anything's better than sitting here waiting for someone to turn up."

So they swung out the barrier that directed the Turnbull Pass traffic into the pub car park. It had a sign on it saying ENQUIRE ABOUT ROAD CONDITIONS AT HOTEL.

A few minutes later a bloke in a van pulled in and came into the bar.

"Is the pass closed?" he asked.

"No, it's just a temporary hold-up," said Arty. "The Ministry of Works is clearing a small slip up there and they don't want the traffic piling up behind them. They're going to ring through when it's cleared. Shouldn't be more than half an hour or so. Would you like a beer?"

"Yes thanks, a Speights."

Their customer was joined a few minutes later by a couple in a car. They were given the same story and didn't question it. They ordered a beer and a gin and tonic. Then two men in a ute came in and listened to Arty's yarn and ordered a jug of beer. Then a truck driver, and four blokes on motor bikes.

After about half an hour Arty announced that the road was open and Joe swung the barrier aside and let the vehicles through. Then he swung it back across the road again and they began on the next batch.

It continued steadily all day, and by the time they closed the pub that night they'd taken more than $800.

"That's more like it," said Arty, putting the money in the pub safe and turning the handle. "If we can keep this up we'll cover the cost of those three kegs in no time."

Business was steady all the next day. Among one lot they caught the Inter-City bus with thirty-five passengers. They spent more than two hundred dollars before Arty and Joe let them go.

The day after that there was a slight hitch. A bloke came into the bar and asked what the barrier was across the road for. Arty looked past him out the window and saw that he was in a Ministry of Works ute.

"I don't know, mate," said Arty. "A bloke rang up a

while back and told us to put the barrier across because of a slip on the pass. We assumed it was one of your blokes."

"Well, there's no slip up there. I've just come through. There's no need to stop the traffic."

"The bastard must have been having us on," said Arty. "Open the barrier, Joe. The road's clear."

"That was dicey," said Arty when everyone was gone. "We'd better leave the road open for the rest of the day in case he comes back. I don't know how much longer we're going to be able to keep this up."

Not much longer, as it turned out. The next day Arty and Joe were entertaining a bunch of clients when Foxy pulled in.

"Here's The Fox!" whispered Arty. "We'd better open the road up."

They had four cars and a truck trapped there at the time. Joe ducked out the back to open up the road. Foxy limped into the bar.

"Okay folks," said Arty loudly. "The road's open. You can go now."

"What's the barrier across the pass road for?" demanded Foxy.

"A slip up on the pass," said Arty. "They get us to stop the traffic down here so it doesn't pile up behind them. They've just rung through that it's cleared."

"I haven't heard of any slip up there," said Foxy suspiciously. "They usually notify me of anything like that."

"It was just a small slip," said Arty. "They probably didn't think it was worth bothering you with."

"I'll be checking out this slip story of yours. I wouldn't put it past you two to stop the traffic just so you can sell your booze."

"Cut it out, Foxy. We wouldn't do a thing like that. It'd be against the law!"

"When did you start worrying about whether anything was against the law or not?" said Foxy. "I'll be checking on this," he repeated as he left the bar.

He got into his car and did a U-turn and drove off up the Turnbull Pass road.

"Well that's that," said Arty. "We can't use that barrier any more. It's too risky with The Fox nosing around like this."

"Do you think he'll really check up on us?" said Joe.

"I wouldn't put it past him. I don't know what they could do to us about it, but if there is anything, Foxy'd find it."

A couple of hours later they saw Foxy come out onto the main road and drive off towards Matea, and an hour or so after that Sergeant Freeman and Cliff James arrived at the Turnbull Tavern in a police car, followed by Foxy in his prowl car.

"Here we go again," muttered Arty. "It's a wonder he didn't bring the Armed Offenders' Squad with him."

The Sergeant led the others into the bar.

"What have you been doing mucking around with the road barrier, Arty? There haven't been any slips on the pass for more than three weeks and you've been holding up the traffic here."

"It's a bloody shame, Sarge," said Arty. "I hope you catch the bastards!"

"What bastards?"

"The bastards who've been ringing up and telling us to stop the traffic because of slips," said Arty. "I think someone's got it in for us, Sarge!"

"Well if it ever happens again I'll have it in for you myself," said the Sergeant. "I'll book you for it."

Foxy was livid.

"You're not accepting that pack of lies, are you Sergeant?

They've been deliberately holding up the traffic to sell their booze! They've had brawls out here! It's nothing but a drunken orgy here, day and night!"

"All right, Foxy," said the Sergeant. "This is a police matter. I'll handle it if you don't mind."

Foxy spun round and stalked out of the bar and drove away, spinning his wheels in the gravel to let them know how hacked off he was.

"Now don't forget, you blokes," said the Sergeant. "Any more of your shenanigans and I'll throw the book at you. And try and keep out of Foxy's road, you know what he's like."

"Whew!" said Joe when the police were gone. "That was lucky!"

"He's a good bloke at heart, the Sarge," said Arty. "But that's the end of our barrier business. We can't risk using it any more now."

"The Fox!" said Joe. "He mucks up everything we try to do."

"I just hope we've made enough to cover the cost of those three kegs," said Arty. "I've lost track of the money side of things. Merv's going to have to sort it out when he gets back."

He needn't have worried about that. When Merv arrived back a couple of days later he was blown away by the amount of money they'd taken.

"This is more than twice as much as I take in a normal week!" he said. "What have you two been up to?"

"Just popular, I guess," said Arty.

Merv paid them a handsome bonus.

"I don't think I'd like to run a pub full-time," said Joe as they drove back to Matea in the ute.

"Nor me," said Arty. "It's too hazardous. But it was a bit of fun while it lasted!"

GRAVE UNDERTAKINGS

ARTY HAD been doing work for the local undertaker for some years, digging graves, mowing grass, and even driving the hearse occasionally. He knew the drill with burials, and one day they offered him a burial of his own.

In a little settlement called Forks, forty-five Ks from Matea, an old bloke called Johnny McNab had been accidentally drowned. Everyone knew Johnny, he'd been left over from the timber-milling days, lived in a caravan at Forks for the past sixteen years. He was to be buried at Forks in the old cemetery, and Arty had been offered the job.

"It's a snip, Joe," said Arty. "There's nothing to it. All we have to do is stick him in a coffin and bury him. Eleven hundred dollars for half a day's work. I've even got a coffin in the shed somewhere. That'll save us having to buy one. And I'm borrowing Dave Cooper's truck to take it out there on."

"What do you want me to do?" asked Joe uneasily.

"I'll need a hand to get him into the coffin and get the coffin into the hole," said Arty. "That's all."

When Joe went round to Arty's place that afternoon Arty had just dragged an old coffin out of a heap of stuff in the corner of the shed. It was painted bright yellow with a big black number 9 on each side. A set of trolley-wheels had been nailed onto it and some old number-plates tacked onto each end of it. Arty set about pulling the wheels off it with a claw-hammer.

"Do you reckon we're going to get that thing cleaned up in time?" asked Joe.

"Sure, we'll slap a coat of that quick-drying paint on it. I've got some here."

"What about a lid for it?"

"I haven't seen one around anywhere," said Arty, "but we can cut one out of a sheet of softboard I've got there. Johnny won't mind."

But it wasn't Johnny they had to worry about. The night before the funeral Arty got a call to say that Johnny had relatives, and some of them were coming down for the funeral.

"They want the procession to leave from the Forks store at eleven o'clock tomorrow morning," Arty told Joe.

"I didn't know Johnny had any relatives," said Joe.

"Nor me," said Arty. "It seems old Johnny had quite a bit of money tied up in a forestry operation up north. His brother is going to help them tidy up the estate, he's an accountant or something."

"Well what do you know? Old Johnny with money behind him! How many of them are coming?"

Arty consulted a piece of paper he had in his pocket.

"Four of them. Johnny's brother Paul, his sister Mavis and her husband Harry. They're bringing a minister with them to conduct the service. The brother sounded all right on the phone."

"Have you been out to the cemetery yet?"

"Yep. I've just got to nick out there later and finish off."

The next morning they set off with the coffin on the back of the truck, with bits of 4 x 2 tacked to the deck to prevent it from sliding around. It was now painted grey, with some cupboard-handles nailed onto it and a softboard lid ready to be tacked on with flatheads. They collected old Johnny from the morgue and put him in the coffin and nailed the lid down and arrived at the Forks store at ten forty-five. Everything was going according to plan.

The hamlet of Forks consisted of a store, an unused garage, a run-down little pub, two houses and a scattering of huts and sheds. A real backwater. It had dwindled to this from a booming community since the timber mill closed down nine years before.

Johnny's relatives and the Minister were waiting there in a big flash car. They were dressed-up and obviously city types. Arty and Joe looked shabby by comparison, despite them having their best gear on. There were a couple of raised eyebrows at the sight of the hearse provided for the occasion but no one said anything. They shook hands all round and Paul, the brother of the deceased, suggested that they get on with it. The deceased's sister, Mavis, and her husband Harry had already got back into the car.

"Okay," said Arty. "Follow us. It's about half a mile to the cemetery."

The two vehicles drove off.

"They've got their lights on," said Joe looking back. "Maybe we'd better turn ours on too."

"Can't risk it," said Arty. "The battery in this thing's getting weak and it's not charging properly. We don't want anything to go wrong."

It had been raining overnight and the wheel-tracks that turned in off the road and led to the cemetery were full of puddles, and the ferns that overgrew the road were still wet. They arrived at the cemetery muddy but without mishap. It was an overgrown scattering of neglected headstones, the fence long-since swallowed up in the fern. The grass was so long and rank that even the cattle had largely given it a miss.

The procession pulled up and they all got out.

"Look at the mess my car's in," said Paul. "I'll never get it clean again!"

"What a terrible old cemetery," said Mavis. "Couldn't we find some place more respectable?"

"It's what John wanted," said Paul.

"Shut up, Mavis," said Harry.

"Give us a hand with this coffin, Joe," said Arty, sliding it to the back of the truck.

They took an end each and began picking their way across the clumpy ground between the headstones.

"Where's the grave?" asked Joe.

"Just over here."

They came to a place where the grass had been cleared away. A shovel and a spade and a grubber were stuck in the bare ground. They put the coffin down. The mourners were coming up behind them.

"Where's the bloody grave, Arty?" hissed Joe.

"I was going to dig it right here," stammered Arty. "I knew I'd forgotten something."

"This is bloody lovely," said Joe. "What are we going to do now?"

"I suppose we'd better get diggin'," said Arty, grabbing the spade and beginning to mark out the grave.

Joe got the shovel and began digging out the earth. The four mourners watched in silence for a few moments, then Paul came over and said, "I say, haven't you even dug my brother's grave yet?"

"We never dig 'em until we're ready to use 'em around here, mate," said Arty without looking up from digging.

"Why not?" said Harry.

"Rather irregular," muttered the Minister.

"It's an old tradition around these parts," explained Arty.

"We never leave open graves lying around, especially at night. The Ngai Tahus'd go berko if we done that. It's supposed to bring terrible bad luck on the whole tribe."

"I've never heard of anything like that," said Harry.

"Most irregular," said the Minister.

"How much longer is this going to take, Harry?" said Mavis, slapping at the calf of her leg. "I'm getting bitten by something."

"Shut up, Mavis," said Harry.

"Are you sure you men are properly authorised to conduct burials?" asked Paul.

"Sure, we've been doin' it for years, eh Joe?"

"Yeah, years," agreed Joe.

The four mourners went into a little huddle some distance off and Arty and Joe went on digging. After about half an hour Arty's spade struck something solid in the bottom of the hole.

"What's this?" he said, scraping dirt away from it.

A bit more scraping soon revealed what it was.

"It's another bloody coffin!" said Joe. "We've dug this grave on top of another one!"

"That's not supposed to be there," said Arty. "I've seen the plans of the cemetery."

"Well it is there," said Joe. "What the hell are we going to do about this?"

"We can't start on another hole," said Arty, glancing across at the restless mourners. "We'll just have to stick him in on top of this one."

So they tidied up the grave, leaving a layer of earth over the coffin in the bottom of it. By this time they were both covered with clay. They dragged the coffin over to the hole and the mourners came and gathered there, anxious to get it over with. Arty and Joe lowered the coffin into the grave. Mavis threw a small bunch of bought flowers onto it.

"I say," said Paul, peering into the grave. "That doesn't look like six feet deep to me."

"It does look a little – shallower than usual," said the Minister.

"That's nothing like six feet," said Harry. "It wouldn't even be five feet, would it?"

"It'll have to be deepened," said Paul.

"Naa, you never want to go any deeper than this around here," said Arty.

"Why not?" said Paul.

"Water, mate. There's water all under here. Go any deeper and she'll fill up with water on you. I've seen us have to drill holes in a coffin and weigh it down with rocks to get it to sink, and that was just over there, eh Joe."

"Just over there," agreed Joe.

"I don't believe that," said Harry.

"Fair go!" said Arty. "There's a spring all under here, eh Joe."

"Yeah, all under here," said Joe. "We can't go any deeper than this," he added truthfully.

"It's still up a bit at this end," said Arty. "I'll just give it a tap down."

He gave the top of the coffin a couple of rams with the shovel, and on the third ram the head of the shovel went through the softboard lid. He quickly wrenched it out, leaving a gaping toothless smile in the coffin lid. The mourners all recoiled into another indignant huddle, not even bothering to keep their voices down any more:

"Beyond a joke!"

"Unheard of!"

"Outrageous!"

"Most irregular."

"Can't we just get this over with?"

"Shut up, Mavis!"

After some further consultation they eventually decided to go with Mavis' idea and get it over with. They approached the grave and the Minister rattled off the ashes and dust bit, and then they picked their way back to their car and turned it round and drove off. Arty and Joe started shovelling the earth back into the hole.

"I hope old Johnny's happy with this," said Arty.

"If he is he's the only one out of that lot," said Joe.

"I wonder if they'll complain or anything?" said Arty.

"There's no need to wonder about that," said Joe. "They've done nothin' but complain ever since they got here. They're not likely to stop now."

"I don't like the look of that brother of his. No wonder Johnny never let on about him."

"We'll just have to wait and see what they do."

They patted the mound of earth flat and put the tools on the truck and drove back down to Forks. The mourners were in yet another huddle beside their car outside the store.

"You coming over to the pub for a beer?" Arty invited.

"No thanks," said Paul. "We'll be getting away, but I think it's only fair to warn you that we're not satisfied with your service. Not at all satisfied. Complaints are going to be laid with the proper authorities as soon as we get back to town."

"And you might as well know that we're applying for an Exhumation Order, so that John can have a decent burial," chipped in Harry.

"Most irregular," intoned the Minister.

"Well in that case you'd better get them to make out your Exhumation Order for two bags of sand," said Arty, "because that's all you'll find in that coffin up there."

"What?" said Harry.

"Do you mean to tell us that John's body wasn't in that coffin?" said Paul.

"You know how Johnny died, don't you?" said Arty.

"Accidental drowning, it was all in the police report."

"Not quite all," said Arty. "Do you know Lake Waitaipo?"

"We passed it on the way down here."

"Do you know it hasn't got any outlet to the sea?"

"So what?" said Paul.

"So it's full of eels. Hundreds of 'em. And you know what happens to land-locked eels, don't you."

"What?" asked Harry.

"They grow real big, that's what. Half as big as a man,

some of 'em, and they get pretty stirred-up when they start feedin'. They get into a frenzy."

"I don't like the sound of this," said Harry.

"What are you trying to say?" said Paul.

"What I'm tryin' to say," said Arty, "is that you don't last long when you drown in Lake Waitaipo. Them eels grab a mouthful of you and start spinnin', and in no time there's nothin' left to fish out."

The Minister mopped his forehead with a handkerchief. Mavis sat back in the open door of the car with her face in her hands.

"I think I'm going to be ill," she said.

"Shut up, Mavis!" said Harry.

"How – how much of him did you . . .?" said Paul.

"Not enough to be worth bringin' out, mate, eh Joe? They're a bit superstitious about buryin' different parts of bodies in different places around here, so we left Johnny in the lake and held his funeral up at the cemetery. It's the way we do things around here."

"Why didn't anybody tell us?" said Paul. "We thought it was just an ordinary drowning."

"Cut it out, mate," said Arty. "We've already had one nervous breakdown over this business around here, and here you go raking it all up again. We've been trying to save you from what we've been through, but if that's the way you want to go, suit yourselves. We done our best."

"Well that certainly explains the – er – irregular procedures," said the Minister.

"Harry, let's go," said Mavis. "I've had enough of this place. I never want to hear about it again."

"Shut up, Mavis," said Harry, getting into the back of the car beside her and shutting the door.

"Look, I don't know what to say," said Paul. "I thought

you two were deliberately being – difficult."

"That's all right, mate," said Arty understandingly. "We've all been through a pretty heavy time over this. Johnny was like one of the family to us. The sooner it's all buried and forgotten about the better."

"Yes, well, thanks anyway," said Paul. "We'll just get going. Are you ready Minister?"

The Minister got into the car beside him and they drove away. Arty and Joe moved off towards the pub for a well-earned beer.

"Bloody hell, Arty!" said Joe. "You sure laid it on a bit thick that time. Do you think they swallowed all that stuff about eels and that?"

"I don't know," said Arty, "but if it stops them goin' up there and disturbin' old Johnny I don't mind stretchin' the truth a bit."

"All we have to do now is hope they don't check up on it," said Joe.

"On the other hand, we've done all right out of it," pointed out Arty. "It's not every day we can make eleven hundred dollars."

"I wouldn't go through that again for eleven thousand dollars," said Joe.

LETTERS

WITH A BAR

JOE DROPPED round to Arty's place one day not long after the undertaking undertaking and found him in a state of excitement. He hadn't seen him for a couple of days.

"Wait till you hear what I've been up to, Joe! I've been waiting to talk to you about it. I think we've bought a business."

"A business? What sort of a business?"

"A road-marking business. That one of Hank Tonk's. Do you know Hank? Lives down in Cemetery Road."

"Seen 'im around. What about him?"

"Well I got talking to him this morning. He's got to sell his road-marking unit and we can have it for a thousand dollars deposit."

"What's it going to cost altogether?"

"Forty-five thousand," said Arty. "It's a bargain!"

"Where's the other forty-four thousand bucks coming from?"

"Work. There's nearly a hundred thousand dollars' worth of road-marking contracts coming up. Hank's prepared to take a percentage of the payments until he's paid off."

"Why's he selling it?"

"His health's packed up on him. He had a weed-spraying outfit before this and the chemicals have got into him. It's made him so crook he can't work any more. He's going to the ACC for compo. I've got to let him know by tonight if we want to take the business over. If we don't, he's going to stick it on the market. What do you reckon Joe?"

"Where are we going to get a thousand dollars from?"

"We've got eleven hundred dollars coming to us from Johnny's burial. We can use that. We've got nothing to lose, Joe. How about it?"

"We can only give it a go," shrugged Joe. "I've got nothing else to do."

"Neither have I," said Arty. "And we can start work as soon as we like. They want that new strip of seal between Donnelly's Gully and the Turnbull bridge marked. Hank or his missus will come out with us and show us what we have to do."

"Well, here we go again," said Joe.

They collected their cheque from the funeral parlour and paid a thousand dollars down on the business and took possession of it. The road-marking unit was a bit of a rumpty outfit. An old two-ton diesel truck with dual rear wheels and two 250-litre paint tanks on the back, and an array of signs and witches' hats and other paraphernalia. Paint-spattered nozzles, pipes and pumps.

Both Carol and Helen were unsupportive of the undertaking, and in the interests of marital harmony Arty and Joe had to agree that if this one failed they would both register for the dole and give up their crazy schemes altogether.

The road-marking business was quite successful at first. There was nothing too complicated about it, the centre lines were marked with tags and easy to follow. A simple computer on the dash worked out the speed and litres-per-kilometer. Then they'd run out a dye-line 3.5 metres from the centre line and paint the edge lines. Joe operated the vehicle and Arty shifted the signs around and directed traffic. He enjoyed the authority it gave him. He especially liked holding up tourist buses and making them pass on the wrong side. Bus drivers don't like the wrong side of the road.

They spent a lot of money paying for paint, which was their main expense. They put in long hours and sometimes had to stay away from home for a few nights, but they made good money and within six months they'd paid off what they owed on the business and Southern Road-marking was freehold. Even Carol and Helen began to relax a little, especially when they were reimbursed for the $1,700 for Arty and Joe's fines over the Great Smell incident.

Then government cut-backs began to reach out to them. They lost a big contract they'd been half-promised because a re-sealing job on Highway 81 had to be cancelled. They finished two short stretches of new seal and suddenly they were scratching. They got what road-marking was available locally but it wasn't enough to keep them going full-time.

They battled on and finally got a contract painting concrete bridges and abutments and they were taking their time on the bridge over Boulder Creek, one of the tributaries of the Turnbull. They were sitting in the wagon eating their lunch. The County blokes were down in the riverbed below them, digging out shingle with a front-end loader and screening it onto trucks to be taken away and spread on the road somewhere. Arty sat watching them.

"There's gold in this river isn't there?" he said.

"Sure," said Joe. "The Turnbull was one of the richest rivers in the country. They're still working it up at Boulder Flat."

"There's got to be gold in that shingle they're putting on the roads," observed Arty.

Joe had spent two years operating a gold-recovery plant and given it up because of the daunting amount of other stuff mixed up with the gold.

"I s'pose there must be," he said absently, munching into an apple.

"That means that thousands of yards of gold-bearing shingle have been dug up and spread out on the roads around here. Millions of yards, in fact. There's got to be gold in it."

"That'd be right, but you'd never find it, " said Joe.

"You might if you ran a gold-detector over it."

"How would you do that?"

"I don't know, but it'd have to be worth a go. Who knows about gold-detectors around here?"

"The Prof might, he's supposed to know all about electronics and stuff."

"That's right, we could try him. I want to find out what those things'll do. I've never had anything to do with them."

Joe was starting to get interested in the idea.

"It certainly wouldn't do any harm to check it out," he said. "I know a bit about gold, but I've never had anything to do with detectors."

"We've got the perfect set-up for finding the gold in the road," Arty pointed out. "We could probably do it while we're marking."

"What do gold-detectors cost, I wonder?"

"We'd have to find out, we might need more than one of them. Let's go and check it out with The Prof and see what he reckons."

"What'll we tell him?"

"We'll just have to take him into our confidence, I suppose. It's a bit of a risk."

"We could tell him we want to use it in the riverbed," suggested Joe.

"Yeah, that'd cover it. We don't want anyone twigging what we're up to. We might just be onto a good thing here!"

"We could tell him we want to mount it on a tractor and drive around the riverbeds," said Joe.

"He might swallow something like that," said Arty. "Let's call in and see him on the way home."

It was said that The Prof had invented something to do with automatic lighthouses and didn't need to work or take a pension, though he'd never displayed any signs of being well-off. He drank for a few hours in the pub every day and then tottered off home with a couple of bottles of wine in a plastic bag. There were rumours that The Prof had been a brilliant academic; he'd had something to do with developing nuclear bombs; he was married to a fabulously-wealthy woman in Auckland; someone was paying him to stay out of some town; he'd inherited a fortune and was drinking his way through it . . . None of these rumours had ever been substantiated. The Prof kept himself and his past to himself.

Joe and Arty called in on him after work that day. They'd seen what you could of his place from the road, but they had no idea what it was actually like. It had been a four-bedroomed house, probably still was, but now it was in a great state of dilapidation. The buckled weatherboards had been painted white with an orange undercoat, now they were grey and peeling, streaked with green drippings from the rusted guttering, a length of which hung down across the front of the house with grass growing in it.

Four turkeys were perched on one of the empty front window-sills, looking outwards. Arty guessed what it was like inside the room. He was partly right. Some kind of vine grew out of the other front window and engulfed one veranda-post and a corner of the roof. The front veranda would be dangerous to walk on and the front door looked like it hadn't been opened for years.

An old red Valiant station-wagon with one front corner

bashed in was parked under the trees, covered with pine needles and bird droppings. It had 'guest wing' painted along one side of it in white paint. They stood for a moment and looked at it. Even Arty was impressed.

"They reckon a gang used to live here before The Prof," said Joe. "I heard he bought the place for a song."

"Looks like it," said Arty.

They picked their way round the side of the house.

"Hell!" said Joe, looking around the neglected yard.

"He must have it the way he wants it," said Arty.

The path to the back door had been laid in bricks. Now the grass grew almost to the middle of it, but it wasn't the grass you had to pick your way through here, it was a magnificent array of wine bottles. They were piled up nearly to the window-sills around the back and sides of the house in a great heap that spilled out across the path. The whole back yard was as overgrown and neglected as the front of the place.

As they reached the back door they could hear someone talking. It turned out to be The Prof, talking to himself.

"Anyone there?" called Arty, knocking on the door.

The talking inside stopped and The Prof came and opened the door. He had a bulging forehead and stomach. He was bald through the middle and wore an old brown knitted jersey and baggy grey pants and red carpet slippers. He had a slight air of suspicion about him, as though visitors usually meant some kind of trouble. He relaxed when he saw it was only Arty and Joe.

"What can I do for you?" he asked. He was always polite.

"You might be able to help us," said Arty. "We want to find out about gold detectors."

"Gold detectors? What do you want to know about them?"

"Well we need to know how they work for a start."

"They're a simple density-detector, aren't they? You can buy them."

"We need one for a special purpose."

"Would you like to come inside?"

"Thanks."

Inside was a shock. The room was filled, every flat surface, with empty wine bottles and pill bottles and magazines. Books and bottles and a great pile of newspapers almost as tall as The Prof in one corner. An old two-bar electric heater cooked the air in the room. The place stank something dreadful and it was only after they'd been in there for a while that they stopped noticing it. The Prof had been living there for eleven years, drinking at least two bottles of plonk a day. Arty figured that there must have been about eight thousand empty wine bottles lying around the place. It was easy enough to believe. He picked up a magazine. It was a science magazine, folded open at an article about something called super-conductors.

They sat on creaking chairs at the old wooden kitchen table. There were at least two dozen wine bottles on the table. They pushed them towards the middle to make room for their elbows.

The Prof offered them a drink, and when they politely refused he said he might just have a wee nip himself, and poured some red wine into a purple-stained glass cup and drank half of it in one gulp. The floor was so uneven that the bottles tinkled every time the table was bumped or someone walked across the sagging floorboards.

"Now what is it you want to know about gold-detectors?" said The Prof, sitting at the table with a tinkle of bottles.

"Everything," said Arty. "We need to know what range

they'll cover, how deep they'll find gold, what speed they'll work at, what they cost."

"I see. What do you actually want to do with it?"

"We want to mount it under a tractor and drive around the riverbed with it," said Joe.

"I see. And what width would you want to cover?"

"About six feet would be enough," said Arty.

"You'd probably need several units to cover that," said The Prof.

"That's what we've come to see you for," said Arty. "We don't know the first thing about it."

"I see. Well I'd have to do some research on it. I could look into it for you if you like."

"We'd be grateful," said Arty. "We don't know where to start."

"You'd have to start by finding out if the idea is theoretically feasible," said The Prof. "I can do that for you. If you come back on Friday I should have the information you need."

"That's real good of you, Prof," said Arty. "We'd appreciate it if you'd keep the idea under your hat for the time being. We don't want anyone else getting onto it."

"Don't worry," said the Prof. "I won't discuss it with anyone else."

Arty and Joe left.

In the three days before Friday they could talk of little else. The more they thought about it the better the idea seemed. They decided not to say anything to their wives about the project in the meantime. They were going to need money to put it together, which meant borrowing money off the bank against their road-marking unit.

After work on the Friday they picked their way through The Prof's magnificent array of bottles and found him passed-out on his bed. He'd overdone it on the plonk. The table had been partly cleared of bottles and was strewn with paper. Figures and diagrams incomprehensible to them.

Arty gave The Prof a shake and he sat up and shouted, "The morphic resonance is incompatible!" then he laid back and passed out again.

"We'll have to come back and catch him before he goes to the pub in the morning," said Joe, pulling a blanket over The Prof. "We're not going to get any sense out of him today."

They found The Prof a bit bleary but wide awake next morning. He sat them down, invited them to have a drop of wine and when they refused he decided to have a wee nip himself.

"How did you go on the research, Prof?" asked Arty.

"Quite well I think. I can't see any reason why you couldn't make up a bar with a series of detectors mounted on it. I've worked out the effective range and depth it should cover. The height above the road is going to be quite critical."

"The road?" said Joe.

The Prof looked at him and smiled and emptied his cup and poured more wine into it and chuckled.

"You knew!" said Joe.

"When two road-markers want a gold detector to mount under a vehicle it isn't very difficult to figure out what they want to do with it," said The Prof. "But don't worry. Your scheme is safe with me."

"Thanks, Prof," said Arty. "What do you reckon it's going to cost us all up?"

"You'd need a bank of detectors, six on the bar to get a scanning overlap, and a hand-held one to pin-point the exact spot where the gold is. They're eight hundred and fifty dollars each. That's about six thousand dollars. The bar would have to be made up. I can supply the specifications for an engineer and mount the detectors on it myself. I'd want to make some minor adjustments to the detectors. They'll run off a twelve-volt system. Seven thousand dollars should be adequate to cover it all."

"How do they actually work, Prof?" said Joe.

"They're quite simple really," said The Prof. "There's a transistorised transmitter and receiver circuit inside the electronics housing, and that's coupled to a transmitter and receiver antenna network housed in the search-head. When the detector is energised an electromagnetic field develops around the transmitting coil. The receiver coil is inductively balanced to the transmitter coil. When a ferrous or non-ferrous metallic object is introduced into the magnetic field an unbalanced condition results between the transmitter and receiver coils. The receiver section simply interprets the unbalanced condition and registers it on a meter or in a speaker, or both."

"Sorry I asked," said Joe.

"How do we go about putting all that together?" asked Arty.

"It shouldn't be very difficult," said The Prof. "I'd have to borrow your vehicle for a day or so to work out what's needed and how to install the unit."

"Not a problem," said Arty. "When do you want it?"

"Well, we could start on it this afternoon if you like," said The Prof, pouring himself another wine.

"We'll bring it round after lunch. Is there anything else you need?"

"An accurate measuring tape, to start with."

"You've got it."

On the Monday Arty and Joe borrowed the money from the bank and then drove up to Danby in Joe's ute with a list of the stuff The Prof wanted, and came back with a load of boxes and cartons and a couple of bottles of wine for The Prof. They had the bar made up and The Prof fixed the detectors onto it and wired them up to the road-marking truck. It wasn't too noticeable among the hoses and nozzles around the vehicle. It was adjustable and could be raised and lowered and slid to stick out three feet on either side of the vehicle. The Prof wired it up to a row of little orange lights in the cab so you could tell which one had been activated. The sound signal came through an amplified speaker under the dash. The Prof accepted fifty dollars for his work, not a cent more. He'd enjoyed doing it. The job had taken the best part of a week and the detector worked fine when they tested it with metal objects.

"It's very crude," said The Prof, "but it should find any gold that's there. You'll have to learn how to interpret the signal responses. I've adjusted it to eliminate as many of the junk items as possible, but you'll have to practise to identify gold signals from other ferrous and non-ferrous items."

They couldn't wait to try it out on the road. They'd been saving a bridge-painting job twenty Ks up a metalled road, and they'd only had the detector-bar turned on for a couple of hundred yards when the bleeper was activated. Arty located the object with the hand-held detector. It was a bolt.

By the time they'd driven out to the bridge and done a couple of hours' painting and then driven back to town at two and a half Ks an hour (the recommended speed), they had half a drum of material on the truck. They had nails and wire and bottle-tops and spent cartridges, nuts and bolts and washers and coins. They also had a fair bit of gravel with something in it that they'd shovelled into the drum to be separated later.

They took it to a creek and put it through a small riffle-box Joe had made up and ended up with five small gold nuggets and two dollars and eighty-five cents in coins. The gold was exciting to find, but it was worth fifty dollars at the most.

"At this rate we're going to have to cover about ten thousand Ks of road to get our money back," said Arty. "At two and a half Ks an hour we wouldn't live long enough."

"We should give it another go," said Joe. "There mightn't be much gold in that particular stretch of road."

"I hope you're right," said Arty. "We can leave the detector on while we're marking roads and hope we pick up the odd decent nugget. That's about the best we can hope for by the look of it."

"It might be worth running it over the road on the way to and from work," suggested Joe.

"It might," said Arty, "but it'd make us hell of a late getting there and getting home again. Depends if it turns out to be worth it. Just as well we haven't told Carol and Helen about it."

"I'll say," said Joe. "Helen'd go berko if she found out we'd borrowed seven thousand bucks to buy a gold-detector. We haven't even paid off our lounge suite yet."

On their way out to another bridge-painting job the next day they decided to run the gold bar over the gravel at the edge of the tar seal. They were confident that nobody would question why the road-markers were crawling along the edge of the road with their orange light flashing, even though they weren't painting anything. They were part of the scene out on the highway. Even traffic cops waved out to them, not counting Foxy.

They had a few flickers that turned out to be metal objects. The metal clip off a pen, some nuts and bolts (mainly off number-plates), the heel off an old leather boot, some bottle tops.

Arty was beginning to think that they'd have been better off driving straight out to the job to make at least a few dollars, when suddenly the bleeper-bank went off with a blast that gave them a fright. Joe stopped the vehicle and reversed back over it. It bleeped and flashed again. Arty hopped out with the hand-detector and immediately located the spot.

"I can see it!" he called out. "It looks like a gold nugget in the tar-seal!"

Joe got out and had a look. It was a piece of gold all right, quite a big one, embedded in the tar among the stones in the surface of the road. They picked it out with the spike of an electric fence standard they had on the truck. It was partly covered with tar but unmistakably gold. It would have half-filled a teaspoon. Joe hefted it in his hand.

"This is about a quarter of an ounce," he said.

"What's it worth?" said Arty peering at it.

"About ninety or a hundred dollars."

"I wonder if there's any more of them?"

"There's only one way to find out," said Joe, putting the nugget in his pocket and heading for the truck. "If there's more nuggets like this in the road we might just have cracked it at last."

They'd only gone about twenty yards when the bleeper activated again. It was another nugget, smaller than the first one. And a few yards on there was another, even smaller. They found five pieces of gold in a two-hundred yard stretch of the road, then there was nothing of gold for miles. They reached the bridge they were supposed to be painting and ate their lunch.

"It looks like the gold is only in certain patches of the road," said Joe.

"That might just be this road," said Arty.

"That's right. It'll probably be different everywhere we

try it, but if we can strike patches like that we're in the money."

"How much do you think we've got so far?"

"About three-quarters of an ounce."

"What's that worth?" asked Arty.

"About three hundred bucks."

"That's good money for a morning's work!"

"It's also the easiest gold I've ever recovered," said Joe. "I reckon we ought to go back and run the bar over that stretch where we found this gold. We only covered one edge of it."

"What about painting the bridge?" said Arty.

"It'll keep. By the time we cover that bit of road properly it'll be time to knock off."

And that's what they did. They set up signs and ran the bar up and down the road until they'd covered it all. They found nineteen pieces of gold altogether. They had to dig into the road a bit in some places to get at buried nuggets, and some of the bleeps were too deep in the tar-seal for them to get at.

There was very little traffic and nobody took any notice of them. They went back to Arty's place and washed the tar off their gold in a pan of petrol. Nineteen bright gleaming pieces of pure gold lying on a tea towel.

"We've got about two and a half ounces of gold here," said Joe. "That's not far off a thousand bucks worth. Good on The Prof! I feel like shouting him a whole crate of plonk, but he'd probably drink himself to death with it."

"Hell!" said Arty, poking at the gold with his finger. "We've struck it rich!"

"We did today," said Joe. "It remains to be seen how it keeps up. It's funny stuff, gold."

Arty was excited. "Are we going to tell the women about it?" he said.

"It might be an idea to leave that until we've paid off our loan," said Joe. "Helen'd be liable to do her block if she found out we borrowed seven grand to build a gold-detector, even if we do have a handful of gold to show for it. Let's just stash this away somewhere until we've got enough to pay the bank off."

"Okay," agreed Arty. "But I can't wait to get out there tomorrow, Joe. Just think of it! Gold in the roads!"

"You'd better settle down before you go inside," laughed Joe. "Carol'd take one look at you and want to know what you've been up to. I'd better get home. See you in the morning."

SLOW
ROAD
NZ 007

Road Works

There was bad news waiting for Joe when he arrived home a bit later than usual. Helen was uptight about something.

"Where have you been?" she demanded. "In the pub I suppose!"

"No, me and Arty had a bit of business to do. What's wrong Honey?"

"I've lost my job. The timber yard's been placed in receivership. We've all been told to finish up at the end of the week."

"Ar, hell!" said Joe. "I'm sorry Honey. Do you think you'll be able to get another job?"

"Around here? You're joking! We've got seventeen per cent unemployment. There just aren't any jobs."

"You could always go on the dole," he suggested.

"Cut it out Joe. I'd go mad with nothing to do all day, you know that."

"Well what are we going to do then?"

"I'll just have to come out and work with you and Arty. I've thought about it, I can drive the ute and put out the signs and bring them up. I know what to do."

"That's okay," said Joe uneasily, "but we haven't got any road-marking to do at the moment. And there's nothing positive coming up that we know about."

"Well what are you doing?"

"Painting bridges and abutments."

"Well I can paint better than you can. Look at this kitchen, I had to go over it after you mucked it up."

"Sure Honey," said Joe, slightly embarrassed at the memory, "but the point is that there just isn't enough work to keep two of us going just now, let alone three."

"Well I'm not sitting at home twiddling my thumbs all day, I'm coming out with you, and that's that, starting on Monday."

He had to agree, he knew her.

"Okay Honey. We can do that until something else turns up."

Joe discussed the situation with Arty the next day.

"Can't you talk her out of it?" asked Arty.

"Not a chance. There's no good reason why she shouldn't come out with us, she's done it before. And you know Helen."

"But she'll find out about our gold detector."

"I know. The best thing for us to do is try to get enough gold to cover what we owe the bank before next Monday."

They got just over an ounce of gold that day, in the stretch of sealed road leading out of town to the west. Once again all the gold seemed to be in one patch of road, except for one good nugget they found on its own. They also got a strong signal from something buried in the middle of the road, right under the white line. They noted where it was, they could dig it out later somehow.

By the end of the week they had three and a half thousand dollars' worth of gold wrapped in the tea towel behind the crates of jars on a shelf in Arty's shed. They drove over to Danby in the ute and sold it to a buyer Joe knew there.

"Well we've half paid-off the detector in a week," said

Joe as they drove back. "That's not bad. Helen can't very well go too crook about that, can she?"

Helen came out on the Monday dressed in blue overalls with a white headband. When they arrived at Arty's place she took one look at the road-marking truck and said, "What's that?" before they'd even got out of the ute.

"What's what?" said Joe uneasily.

"All those round things under the road-marking truck. They weren't there before."

"Oh that. That's a metal detector we had made."

"You had it made? What for?"

"Finding gold in the roads."

"Gold in the roads? What did that thing cost?"

"About seven grand."

"Where did you get the money, Joe?"

"Borrowed it from the bank."

"You borrowed seven thousand dollars to build a thing to find gold in the roads?" She was starting to throw sparks in among her words.

"We've already found some . . ."

"You put us back in debt for that gadget? Just when we were starting to get our heads above the water? And now I've lost my job? And you haven't got any marking work?"

"We've only had it for a week and we've already found enough gold to pay off half of it."

"And how did this gold get in the road in the first place?"

"It's all through the gravel they make the roads with around here. We've been finding some good nuggets, Honey."

Helen wasn't impressed. "You went and put us in debt for seven thousand dollars for one of your crazy schemes?"

"Come on, Honey. It'll be paid off in no time. We have to make money somehow. There hasn't been enough work coming in to keep us going, you know that. We made three and a half thousand dollars with gold last week. In another week or so we'll be in the clear, if we get a bit of luck. You'll see."

Helen still refused to be impressed. Arty came out and they got into the truck and drove off in stony silence. It didn't pay to say too much to Helen when she was in that mood.

They went out to the bridge they should have painted last week and got Helen started on it. Then the men prospected the road beyond that, returning at lunch time with four pieces of gold and a promising patch of road to cover in the afternoon. They showed the pieces of gold to Helen, who was by this time more inclined to listen to them about gold in the roads.

"How much is this worth?" she said, examining the tarry nuggets.

"About a third of an ounce. A hundred and twenty or thirty dollars. We could double that this afternoon if we get lucky."

"I hope you're right," said Helen, handing the gold back to Joe. "In the meantime at least one of us is doing an honest day's work."

It took Helen three days to paint the bridge, which was at least a day faster than Joe and Arty would have done it. By this time the men had covered all the road within striking distance of the bridge and found about a thousand dollars worth of gold. The bridge-painting job was worth two hundred and seventy-five dollars, less tax. Helen was silenced, but still a bit sceptical.

On the Friday they decided to start prospecting the Eastern Highway. Helen followed them out in the ute with the signs and they worked their way along, stopping to put out the signs and prospect the whole road whenever they found gold along the edges.

They got a positive reading from something out in the road, right in the approach to a bridge. They held up the traffic while they dug a hole in the road with their spike but whatever it was, it was too deep. They packed the tarred gravel back into the hole and let the traffic go. They would have to leave it for another time.

That day they found an ounce and three-quarters of gold, including one nugget nearly half an ounce. By this time Helen was completely won over to the operation. They were getting practised at identifying the bleep of gold from the bleep of other things. The gold bleep was sharper and more positive. In loose gravel they found that the slower they went the smaller the flakes of gold they could find. Arty gathered the bleeps on the shovel and put them in the drum on the truck to be separated later. All the rubbish went into another drum.

You could find a piece of gold anywhere and they prospected wherever they could. They'd already found two bleeps in the road between Joe's place and Arty's, and there was a beauty down by the County Depot gate. Even gateways, pull-overs, rest areas and gravel pits could have gold in them.

Within three weeks they'd paid off the gold-bar and covered more than one hundred and fifty Ks of local roads. They figured that there were one-and-a-half thousand Ks of gold-bearing road in the region. Helen marked off the places they'd done on a map and noted the spots where the road needed digging up to get at the gold. There were already more than a dozen places that they reckoned were worth investigating.

Digging into tar-seal wasn't easy, either. After a bit of experimenting they found that the best way to crack the seal was to hammer a big steel chisel into the road and lever out the chunks of seal with it and run the detector over them until they had the piece of gold or whatever else it might be.

They had a gas cooker on the truck for melting small blocks of bitumen for installing cats-eyes in the roads. They could easily make up a brew to repair the holes they dug if they needed to, but in most cases the already-tarred gravel could be rammed back into place as firmly as it was before they dug it up.

They could get away with just about anything with the road-marking truck, the signs, Helen with her flaming red hair and orange Day-Glo road-safety vest, but digging holes in perfectly good tar-sealed roads was going to take a bit of subtlety.

They'd got two plastic gold pans and by halving the material they shovelled or dug up and running the hand detector over it they could get right down to the gold simply and quickly. That was a part of the operation they had to be particularly careful about. It would have been too hard to explain away if they were caught using gold pans. They kept them hidden behind the seat of the truck when they weren't being used.

As the weeks went by and they became more expert at identifying the signals from the detector, they could cover the ground at five Ks an hour, twice the speed The Prof originally recommended. Joe, especially, could tell the flicker of a gold flake or the tickle of a trace or the bleep of a small nugget or the zing of a big one, and roughly how deep in the road they were. They were recovering between $1,500 and $4,000 worth of gold from the roads around Matea every week, and there was a lot of road still to prospect.

"We're going to have to watch The Fox," remarked Joe as he and Helen and Arty passed him as they drove out to the job one morning. "He'd have us up like a shot if he found out what we're up to. I don't think he's ever forgiven us for getting away with dropping that tree on his car."

"Someone saw him in an unmarked car yesterday," said Arty. "It's a grey Commodore."

"We'll have to watch out for that," said Joe.

"What could he have us up for?" said Helen.

"I don't know," said Arty, "but if there is anything, Foxy's just the bloke to find it."

Later that day, when they were prospecting a promising stretch of the Eastern Highway, The Fox cruised past in the unmarked grey Commodore and slowed down to a crawl as he passed them, staring at them and their outfit. Arty gave him a wave and he raised his fingers on the steering-wheel in reply and sped off.

"Unfriendly sort of a coot," said Joe.

"He's nosy, isn't he!" said Helen.

"He's dangerous," said Arty. "We've got to make sure he never catches us digging up the road. We'd better post a lookout for him whenever he's around."

Foxy continued to be a worry. He had a habit of turning up unexpectedly in all sorts of places at any old time. Early or late, you could run into him anywhere. He rang the police one night and told them that they were selling beer out the back door of the pub after hours, but the police got there too late to apprehend anyone. He gave the Fire Service Chief's wife a ticket for parking in front of the Fire Station. He stopped Carol one morning on her way to the school to make sure the kids were wearing seat-belts. He stopped a bunch of youngsters on their way to a twenty-first one Saturday night and breath-tested the driver and poured all their beer and wine down the gutter. He had old Gordon Rogers up for not having reflectors on his push-bike, when Gordon hadn't been out after dark for years. He prosecuted everyone he could for everything he could. He was a ratbag, and he stalked Southern Road-marking as though they were doing something suspicious. In fact he stalked everyone as though they were doing something suspicious.

Even old Father Formby, bless him, a man who had never been known to say a bad word about anybody, was heard to observe one day that "Mr Fox seems rather lacking in Divine attributes".

One of his stunts involved Sergeant Freeman and Cliff James. He passed them in a police car one day and noticed that they weren't using seat belts. He turned round and caught up to them and put the siren on and stopped them and gave them tickets for failing to wear seat belts.

On court day the Sergeant and Cliff both pleaded guilty and got a lecture from the magistrate about what a bad example they were to the community.

"If the police themselves don't wear seat belts we can only expect others to flout this law as well," he said.

He fined them each seventy-five dollars and twenty dollars costs.

The Sergeant was grim on Foxy over that.

They were prospecting another stretch of the Eastern Highway one day when The Fox cruised past without looking or returning Arty's wave.

"Damn it!" said Joe. "Bloody Foxy."

"Shall I follow him in the ute and see where he goes?" suggested Helen.

"No, you couldn't warn us in time if he decided to double back," said Arty. "We'll have to suspend operations until he's gone back to town. He's got to come back this way."

"Here he comes back again already," said Helen.

"Give me that chisel," said Joe. "I'll hide it in the cab."

Foxy swung in and pulled up behind the road-marking truck and got out and limped around it, taking everything in.

"What can we do for you, Foxy?" said Arty.

"What are you supposed to be doing out here?" said Foxy. "This road's already been marked."

"We're checking for faulty and missing cat's-eyes and reflector-posts at the moment," said Arty.

"Who authorised you to do that?"

"It's part of a general maintenance programme we carry out when we're not marking," said Arty.

"What's that gadget under your truck there?"

"It's a metal detector," said Arty. "We pick up all sorts of rubbish off the roads, look," and he showed Foxy the drum two-thirds full of wire and chain and nails and cans and foil and glass and . . .

"Did this all come off the road?" said Foxy, peering into the drum.

"Yep," said Arty. "It can be dangerous, some of that stuff. That's why we like to clear it off the roads."

Foxy was still suspicious.

"Who authorised you to do this?" he repeated.

"When did you need authority to pick up dangerous rubbish off the road?" said Arty. "We happen to be professional about our work. We do the best job we possibly can."

"Who authorised you to do this work?" insisted Foxy.

"No one," said Arty.

"Then what are you doing here?"

"Research," said Arty.

"What sort of research?"

"Look, Foxy," said Arty, suddenly deciding to take him into their confidence. "We've got this plan to offer them a complete road-grooming and maintenance service for the various sections of highway. We mark them and mow them and keep them clear of rubbish and carry out all minor maintenance work. The way it is they've got different outfits doing the different jobs, we reckon we can save them money and do a better job . . . Don't let on to anyone about this, Foxy," he added. "We don't want anyone else getting onto the idea before we're ready."

"That still doesn't explain what you're doing here," said Foxy, peering again into the drum of rubbish. "What's this research you're going on about?"

"We're working out our costs-per-kilometer at the moment," said Arty. "As you know, some stretches of road need more maintenance than others. We have to do our research before we can put in our prices, just like everyone else has to."

"You can't go obstructing a public highway like this without the proper authority," said Foxy. "You can't go putting up signs whenever you like."

"Well I don't know how we're supposed to do a professional job and train new staff then," said Arty indignantly. "You had to be trained out on the road, didn't you? What about our staff?"

"What staff?" said Foxy. "I don't see any new staff."

"Who do you think this is?" said Arty, pointing at Helen.

"Who is it?" said Foxy.

"Our new operator," said Arty. "We're thinking of putting another unit on the road, once we get going, and we'll need experienced staff to operate it."

"A woman?" said Foxy.

"What's wrong with that?" demanded Helen.

"Nothing, I suppose," said Foxy. "But I still don't think you can obstruct a highway like this without the proper authorisation."

"No," said Helen. "What do you mean by that, a woman?"

"It's not the kind of work a woman ought to be doing," said Foxy. "It's men's work."

"Are there any women traffic cops?" demanded Helen. "Are there?"

"There are some, but that's different."

"What's different about it? Come on, what's different about it?"

Arty and Joe knew not to chip in by this time. Helen was getting fired up, her words as red as her hair.

"It's a different kind of work, that's all," said Foxy. "You can't compare it."

"Are you trying to say that it's harder to paint roads than be a traffic cop? Are you?"

"I don't believe that women ought to be traffic officers either, if you must know," said Foxy.

"You're prejudiced!" accused Helen. "You're prejudiced against women!"

"I'm prejudiced against anyone who doesn't conform to the regulations," said Foxy primly. "It's my job."

"Then why don't you run away and find somebody not conforming to your precious regulations and let us get on with our work," she snapped, dismissing him with a wave of her hand. "If you're not busy, we are."

Foxy was beginning to realise that he was losing ground. He began to move towards his car.

"I'll have to look into this," he said. "You'll be hearing from me about it."

He climbed into his car and buckled his safety-belt and drove off in the direction of Matea.

"He's a nasty customer, that one," said Joe as they watched Foxy disappear. "Do you think he fell for that yarn of yours about maintenance and all that?"

"I don't know," said Arty, "but we'll have to be extra

careful of The Fox now. Just keep a look-out in case he comes back and I'll dig this nugget out of the road here. Where's the chisel, Joe?"

They didn't see much of Foxy for a couple of weeks after that. He drove past them a few times but didn't slow down or even look at them. Arty always waved out to him, which he pretended not to see.

"He makes me nervous, that bloke," said Arty, when Foxy had just driven past one day.

"He gives me the creeps," said Helen. "The other day he drove past and left Tracy Burke broken down with the three kids in the car."

"He's put Tommy Bannister's septic tank truck off the road," said Arty. "Tommy can't afford to get it done up for a warrant."

"That truck of Tommy's has never had a warrant yet, has it?" said Joe. "How's he managing?"

"He's not," said Arty. "It's put him out of work."

"That wouldn't worry The Fox," said Joe.

No, nothing seemed to worry Foxy. He carried on doing everything exactly by the book and hacking off everyone. He was almost fanatical about alcohol, and breath-tested everyone who might conceivably have been drinking, and caught quite a few of them. Like most of the regulars, Arty and Joe didn't go to the pub much any more. If they wanted a beer they usually bought some and drank it at home, or in Arty's shed, where a home-brew was fermenting.

With most of the older cars off the road and the pub carpark practically empty, the little town was strangely subdued. It became a local practice that if you saw Foxy anywhere you flicked your headlights at the approaching traffic to warn them. Foxy responded to this by handing out Traffic Offence Notices for headlight-flicking.

Foxy didn't get off scot-free over all this. He'd already complained to the police a few times about things people were doing to him. Someone was putting a stack of empty booze bottles outside his front gate every couple of days. Then someone chained the back axle of his patrol car to the post his letterbox was on and when he drove out he broke the post off and dragged half his front fence down.

Then, in response to an anonymous tip-off, the police paid Foxy a visit and found two brand-new chainsaws under his house. They'd been stolen that week from Frazer's Hardware Store. It was rumoured that Foxy had quite a time talking his way out of that one. Next thing Foxy's personal Commodore was up on the hoist in the garage, where they found that someone had put a handful of grinding-paste in his differential and it was chewed-out. The public turned out to be singularly unhelpful to the police with their enquiries regarding these offences and none of them had, as yet, been resolved. Just about everyone in Matea had a motive for doing these things to Foxy.

In the meantime Foxy continued hassling the good citizenry of Matea, like a shark feeding on a school of herrings. Arty summed it up one day when he said, "Matea's too small for The Fox, he needs a whole city to prey on."

Sprung

It was about a month since their confrontation with Foxy out on the Eastern Highway. Joe and Helen arrived at Arty's place one morning to find that Cliff James had just left there. He'd delivered a summons for them to appear at the District Court at ten o'clock the following Thursday to answer charges of illegal use of road signs and obstructing a public highway.

"They can't do that!" said Helen indignantly. "He didn't even give us a ticket!"

"They're doin' it," said Arty. "Foxy could write out a ticket for anything he liked and throw away the top copy and say he gave it to us."

"What are we going to do about it?" said Joe.

"We'll have to stick to our story," said Arty. "They couldn't do much more than fine us for that, could they?"

"I don't trust that Foxy," said Helen.

"Neither do I," said Carol. "What if he finds out about the gold?"

"That's something that mustn't happen," said Arty. "We've got away with it so far, but we have to be extra careful not to get caught, especially by The Fox."

"Maybe we ought to give up the gold prospecting for a while," suggested Joe.

"Not a bad idea," agreed Arty. "The contract's coming up next week for us to re-mark the Western Highway out to the county boundary. That'll keep us busy for a while. Meantime we can only turn up in court on Thursday and see what they do to us."

On the Thursday they sat through a whole morning of court cases, most of them minor traffic offences. Foxy stood up and gave his evidence as though he was reading it out of a book. Fine after fine was imposed, with a couple of excess-alcohol cases that involved a six-month loss of licence as well as a fine.

The magistrate adjourned the court for lunch and they had to come back in the afternoon. Theirs was the second case called. Arty and Joe and Helen stood there. The clerk read out the charges.

"Illegal use of road signs and obstructing a public highway."

"Do you have a lawyer?" asked the magistrate.

"No sir," said Arty.

"Very well. You may proceed, Mr Fox."

Foxy stood up and said that on the date in question he'd become suspicious of Southern Road-marking's operation when he was on patrol and questioned the defendants. Their replies to his questions had been evasive, but he'd established that they were putting up signs and diverting traffic without authority. This was clearly in violation of the law relating to the obstruction of public roads, as set out in Amendment C of the Traffic Regulations, 1978. He concluded by saying that the defendants' attitude had been uncooperative. Then he sat down.

"Have you got any reply to these charges?" said the magistrate to Arty and Joe and Helen.

"Yes sir," said Arty.

And he told them the one about how they were trying to evolve a more efficient and safer system for marking and grooming the roads; how they'd been simply practising and perfecting some new techniques for road-marking and maintenance, and training new operators; how they'd retrieved tons of rubbish from the roads using their own invention and at their own cost. The magistrate interrupted him.

"Thank you Mr Brown," he said. "How long have you been operating the road-marking business?"

"On and off for years," lied Arty. "Can't remember off-hand."

Joe saw Cliff James give a slight start when Arty said that, but he was on their side and relaxed back into his chair.

"Mr Fox?" said the magistrate.

Foxy stood up.

"These people are professional road-markers. Was there anything dangerous about what they were doing on this occasion?"

"Not exactly, Your Honour, but the law is quite clear on it. Amendment C clearly states . . ."

"Thank you, Mr Fox," interrupted the magistrate, beginning to shuffle papers on his desk. "All day," he went on, "I've been hearing a string of cases that are so petty that I wonder whether a warning might not have been a more appropriate method of dealing with many of them. I can't allow the court's time to be taken up with misdemeanours of this nature. This case is dismissed, and I'm adjourning the court until next Thursday to give the police time to reconsider pursuing all of these remaining charges." And he stood up and left the room, obviously hacked-off.

Foxy caught up with Arty and Carol and Joe and Helen out on the street. He was furious, and looked it. He was showing some sort of emotion.

"I know you lot are up to something," he hissed so that

no one else could overhear him. "I don't know what it is, but I'll find out, and when I do . . ."

"What are you picking on us for?" demanded Helen impatiently. "Why don't you just leave us alone, instead of hanging around like a bad smell all the time?"

"You lot have got a cheek talking to anyone about bad smells, after what you've done in this town," said Foxy. "You're just lucky you weren't responsible for an outbreak of cholera or something over that."

"That was weeks ago," said Arty. "What do you want to go dragging that up for?"

"I don't forget things like that," said Foxy. "And I'll tell you something else – just because you've got the Sergeant in your pocket you needn't think you're going to go on getting away with thumbing your noses at the law. I'm going to put you where you belong if it's the last thing I do."

"Well just let me tell you something, Mister fusspot Fox," said Helen. "Everyone around here is heartily sick of you and your stupid nit-picking. There isn't anyone in this whole valley who can stand the sight of you. You're nothing but a measly misanthropist!"

You could see that Foxy didn't know what that meant, but he knew it wasn't a compliment.

"Can't you control your wife?" said Foxy to Joe. "She can't go talking to an officer of the law like that."

"You control her," said Joe. "You started it."

"Oh go away, you nasty little thing," said Helen loudly so other people on the street could hear. "Go and pester somebody else for a change!"

"I'm just doing what I'm paid to do," said Foxy, "and no one's going to get away with anything while I'm in charge around here." And he stalked away because people were beginning to stare at them.

"Hell!" said Joe. "How would you like to be like him?"

"No thanks," said Arty.

"Ugggh!" shuddered Helen.

"I wonder if he's got any friends?" said Carol.

"Can't imagine it," said Joe.

"Cliff James told me the other day that the police have already told Foxy to lay off charging people with petty offences," said Arty. "And he sure got off-side with the magistrate in there today."

"Do you think it might make him more lenient on people?" said Carol.

"Na," said Joe. "Not the way he was talking just now."

"Yeah," agreed Arty. "It sounds like he's really got it in for us."

They re-marked the Western Highway, surreptitiously prospecting it for gold at the same time. No one passing realised how often they were stopping. By this time the gold-bar and detectors were spattered with paint, which camouflaged them among all the other paint-spattered paraphernalia on and around the truck. The prospecting was patchy but quite rich in places and they were doing all right for themselves.

The Fox cruised past a few times, and one day he parked in a lay-by and watched them for a while. There wasn't much gold in that stretch of road anyway.

Another time he turned up when they were digging up some tar-seal to get at a nugget. Helen warned them just in time for Joe to get the truck parked over the hole. Foxy stopped and walked over to them.

"What's going on here?" he said.

"What do you mean, what's going on?" said Arty.

"Why are you stopped here?"

"Our line's getting a bit fuzzy around the edges, if you

haven't noticed," said Arty. "We're changing our nozzle."

"What's taking you so long to get this job done?" said Foxy. "It should have been finished days ago."

"We've been having a run of minor hold-ups and breakdowns," said Arty. "There's no law against that, is there?"

"It's about time you got yourselves a new outfit," sneered Foxy. "This one's obviously on its last legs."

"We would if we could afford it," said Joe.

"Well get on with it," said Foxy, moving away towards his car. "I'll be putting in a report about the inefficiency of your operation."

"Do you think he's serious about reporting us?" said Helen when Foxy had gone.

"Wouldn't put it past him," said Joe.

"Let's get this nugget," said Arty. "We'll worry about Foxy later."

They got Helen to park up on the corner to warn them if The Fox came back, while Arty and Joe dug their nugget out of the road and patched up the hole.

Helen was almost full-time watching out for Foxy these days, while Arty and Joe recovered the gold. They couldn't have got away with it without her. There was a bit of a thrill in it for all of them.

That week they made $1,500 for road-marking and $3,500 for gold, seven ounces of it.

"Right under Foxy's nose!" said Arty.

There wasn't much doing for a while after that. A spell of dirty weather kept them off the road for nearly a week. Then one morning Joe rang Arty to tell him they'd just seen Foxy heading off down the Southern Highway.

"It might be a good day to go out and finish off on the Western Highway," said Arty. "The weather looks like it's settled down."

"That's what we were thinking," said Joe.

There were four good bleeps on the Western Highway that they'd had to leave because of heavy traffic or Foxy hanging around. They drove out and located the first one. It was right under the white line in the centre of the road.

The traffic was light. They parked the truck in the middle of the road with the orange light flashing and put up signs and dug out the zing. It was buried about nine inches deep in the road and turned out to be half a horse-shoe. They threw it into the rubbish drum and filled in the hole and repainted the white strip with a brush. And they were just waiting for the paint to dry when The Fox came round the bend in his prowl car and pulled up behind them and came round looking all business-like.

"What are you doing here?" he demanded.

"We're touching-up," said Arty.

"What do you mean, touching-up?"

"Touching-up our road-marking job," said Arty. "Not all the surface takes the paint properly. We have to go back over it and touch it up by hand in some places."

"You must have been already paid out for this job, haven't you?"

"Yes, we have as a matter of fact."

"Then they must have been satisfied with the job."

"They might have been, but we're not," said Arty. "Some of these porous spots only fade off after the job's been inspected."

Foxy peered at the freshly-painted white strip. "I didn't know that," he said. "How long is it going to take you to finish this touching-up?"

"Depends," said Arty. "We could finish it today if we get left alone to get on with it."

"Well do that," snapped Foxy. "I'll be looking into this touching-up business."

He got into his car and backed around and drove back towards Matea.

"He only came out here to check up on us," said Helen.

"He nearly caught us, too," said Arty. "If he'd turned up a few minutes earlier he'd have found us with the road dug up. That would have taken a bit of explaining!"

They posted Helen on look-out and located and dug up the three other bleeps and got three nice pieces of gold. Worth coming out for. They didn't see any more of The Fox that day, in fact they didn't see much of him at all for the next couple of weeks. It almost seemed as though he'd decided to leave them alone.

They painted a couple of bridges and sneaked in a bit of prospecting, and it was on one of these bridge-prospecting jobs that they ran across the richest patch of road they'd found yet. It was just up the Boulder Creek Road, in sight of the main highway. There was a hundred-yard stretch of the road with gold all through it. They could hardly believe it at first, they thought something must have gone haywire with the detector. When they drove over that patch of road it crackled and fluttered and flashed and bleeped and zinged, all at once.

"Hell!" said Joe. "The road here must be full of bloody gold!"

"It must be," agreed Arty. "There must be ounces in here, but we'd have to dig up the whole road to get it, and we're not geared up for an operation that size. We're going to have to leave it here."

They drove back to where Helen was painting a bridge and brought her to have a look at what they'd found. She could hardly believe it either.

"How much do you think is under here?" she said.

"Thousands of dollars' worth," said Joe.

"And it's going to have to stay there until Foxy gives us permission to dig up the whole road and put it through a screening-plant," said Arty.

"You mean forever?" said Helen.

"Looks like it," said Arty. "But it's nice to know it's there."

That rich piece of road became known to them as the Boulder Creek Deposit.

They decided that they'd have to invest in some security measures to combat Foxy's foxiness. They bought and rigged up a radar-detector in the truck, but it only worked in one direction and The Fox would have to have his radar turned on. It only alerted them once, and they weren't doing anything naughty at the time.

Two two-way radios they bought were more effective. Helen could patrol the area in the ute and warn Arty and Joe when she saw Foxy.

"Foxy! Two and a half Ks south, heading in your direction. Plain car!"

Foxy became more suspicious than ever. Every time he was anywhere near where the road-marking truck was, he and Helen kept passing each other on the road. He stalked them and she stalked him, and Arty always waved out to him when he went past, which deepened Foxy's resolve to find out what 'that lot' were up to.

Why would anyone drive aimlessly up and down the same stretch of road with a ute-load of road signs? It was no use questioning them, they'd only hand him another pack of lies. He was going to have to try something different. He did, and that's how he caught them.

They were out on the Southern Highway this day, digging out some gold they knew was there. They'd heard that Foxy was going to be tied up in court all day, so they left the ute at home and the three of them were in the road-marking truck. They'd done four blips and got four nice pieces of gold. They finished another hole, in which they found a small nugget, and patched up the road and moved on. Just around the bend there was a metalled rest area.

"We'd better run the bar over this rest area up here," said Joe. "We haven't done it yet."

They swung into the rest area, and there, half out of sight behind some flax bushes and shrubs, was Foxy's grey Commodore. They stopped.

"I don't like the look of this," said Arty.

"Where's Foxy?" said Joe.

"There he is," said Helen.

Foxy came limping down the hill and climbed the fence and came across to the road-marking truck, hefting a pair of binoculars in one hand. They got out of the truck and stood there.

"Digging stuff up out of the roads, eh!" said Foxy, almost grinning. "I knew you lot were up to something with that metal detector. Gold, is it?"

"We do get the odd flake," admitted Arty. "There's nothing wrong with that, is there?"

"We'll be seeing all about what's wrong with it," said Foxy grimly. "In the meantime I'm impounding this vehicle and its contents. You can either follow me to the Police Station, or I can get the police out here to arrest you."

"We'll follow you," said Arty resignedly.

They drove back towards Matea, Foxy in front and the road-marking truck dawdling along behind.

"Well, that's that," said Arty. "We're sprung."

"That bloody Foxy!" said Joe. "Someone's going to knock the bastard off one of these days!"

“What will we do now? said Helen.

“It’s out of our hands now,” said Arty. “The least we can expect is a healthy fine. I can’t see what else they can do to us, but it’ll put a stop to our operation. How much gold have we got here?”

Helen took a folded piece of paper out of the glovebox and opened it up.

“Five pieces,” she said.

“We’ll have to get rid of that,” said Arty. “They might search us. We don’t want them to find out how much of it we’ve been getting. Keep one piece to account for the hole Foxy saw us dig. The smallest one.”

“What are we going to do with the rest of it?” said Joe.

“Here, give it to me,” said Arty. “Pull over towards the side when Foxy goes out of sight on this corner up here, and I’ll drop it into the gravel at the edge of the road. We can find it again later when we get the chance.”

They did that, and followed Foxy into town, where he directed them to park in the alleyway beside the Police Station.

Cliff James was on his own at the station, typing something at a desk.

“I’m charging these three with wilful damage to a public highway,” said Foxy. “They’ve been digging up the roads.”

“Digging up the roads?” said Cliff incredulously.

“They’ve been digging gold up out of the roads. They admitted it. They’ve got a metal detector rigged up under their road-marking truck. I knew all the time they were up to something!”

“What are you actually charging them with?” asked Cliff.

“Wilful damage to a public highway will do for a start. There’ll be other charges.”

"Where is this damage?" said Cliff.

"I saw them doing it," said Foxy. "They've been doing it all over the place!"

"Show me the damage and I'll charge them."

Foxy was getting rattled. "Damn it, Cliff," he said. "I saw them doing it with my own eyes. They've admitted it!"

"Where?"

"Out on the Southern Highway."

"Well I'd better go and have a look at it," said Cliff.

"Where's Sergeant Freeman?" demanded Foxy.

"He's out on an investigation with Constable Scott," said Cliff formally. "You can wait for them if you like."

"Are you going to charge these people or not?" demanded Foxy impatiently.

"I want to see the evidence first," said Cliff.

"All right," said Foxy. "I'll show you. Come with me."

They piled into Foxy's car, Arty, Joe and Helen in the back, and drove out to where they'd dug up their last nugget.

Foxy parked the car and they all got out.

"Where's the damage?" said Cliff.

"Just over here. They dug a big hole in the road and filled it in again."

"They filled it in?"

"Yes. It was right over here somewhere."

Arty and Joe and Helen could see where they'd rammed the tarred gravel back into place, but it was barely discernible.

Foxy was looking around ten yards away from it.

"Where?" said Cliff.

"Damn it, Cliff. I don't know. They've filled it in again. But I saw them dig a big hole right in the road here. They're not getting away with going around doing that!"

"I can't charge them without any evidence," said Cliff.

"I want to see the Sergeant about this," said Foxy.

"You're welcome," said Cliff. "He should be back by now."

So they got back into the car and drove in silence to the Police Station. Sergeant Freeman and Constable Scott were there and Cliff explained the situation to them.

"And Cliff refused to charge them," added Foxy.

"Have you been doing this, Arty?" said the Sergeant.

"Doing what, Sarge?"

"Using a metal detector and digging up the roads to get gold?"

"Not much," said Arty. "The detector's mainly for finding rubbish, but we do run across the odd piece of gold. It's a bit of a perk."

"You can't go obstructing traffic and digging up stuff out of the roads," said the Sergeant. "I want that detector taken off that truck before it goes out on the road again, you understand?"

"Okay, Sarge," said Arty.

"Just a minute," said Foxy. "They're not getting off like that. I want that vehicle impounded as evidence."

"No, Foxy," said the Sergeant. "We're not laying any more of your petty traffic offence charges. You heard the Judge the other day."

"Petty?" said Foxy. "You call this petty? . . . I'm going over your head on this, Sergeant. I'll be reporting directly to my superiors about it."

"Please yourself," said the Sergeant.

Foxy stalked out of the station.

"I'm blowed if I know what to do about you two," said the Sergeant to Arty and Joe. "You can't raise a few chooks like everyone else, you have to try and raise five hundred of the bloody things, and disrupt the whole neighbourhood. You can't grow a crop of cabbages without upsetting everyone around and polluting the river. You can't collect rubbish without making one hell of a mess. You can't cut a tree down without wrecking a police car. You can't dig a hole in the ground without endangering lives and the health of everyone in the town. You can't run a pub for a few days without causing brawls and obstructing traffic. And now you're running around digging up the roads. Can't you do anything without mucking it up?"

"We've had a bad trot, Sarge," said Arty. "But our road-marking operation's been going all right, hasn't it?"

"It's not a very good average, Arty. If you keep this up I'm just going to have to lock you up before you hurt someone. You heard what the magistrate said last time. I'm getting sick of squaring off for you."

"We're only trying to make an honest crust, Sarge," said Arty. "It's not easy these days."

"You'd better get that detector off your truck," sighed the Sergeant. "And keep out of Foxy's way."

"We've been trying to," said Arty. "He won't leave us alone."

"Well get out of here, and no more digging up the roads, okay?"

"Okay, Sarge," said Arty, leading the way out of the office.

They got into the truck and backed out and drove off.

"Whew!" said Arty. "We were lucky that time!"

"You're not kiddin'," said Joe. "I thought we were going to end up in the clink, one part of it!"

"We would have, if Foxy had his way," said Helen. "He could still cause trouble for us yet."

"That's right," said Arty. "And in the meantime he's put the knockers on our gold operation."

They went to Arty's place and told Carol, who was just home from the school, what had happened.

"That horrible man!" she said. "What's he going to do next?"

"We'll just have to wait and see," said Joe. "He might get transferred somewhere else, or drop dead," he added.

The next day they disconnected the gold-bar and unbolted it off the truck and stashed it in Arty's shed. Then they went down and put in their price for installing reflector posts on the Southern Highway. They wouldn't know if they'd got the job for about three weeks.

"Now we can only sit back and wait for events," said Arty.

A Favour from the Fox

Two weeks after they'd been caught, Cliff James arrived round at Arty's place, where Arty and Joe were re-stacking a pile of timber they'd backed the truck into and knocked over when they were taking the gold-bar off.

"G'day, Cliff!" said Arty. "What have we done now?"

"You'd know that better than me," grinned Cliff. "I've got a message for you blokes and Helen."

"I bet it's about those couple of bits of gold we dug out of the road," said Arty.

"That's right. They want you to attend a meeting."

"That bloody Foxy!" said Joe. "What's he up to now?"

"I don't know," said Cliff. "We've been told to set up a meeting tomorrow morning at the Court House at eleven o'clock and they want you three to be there. That's all I know about it."

When Cliff had gone, Joe said, "I wonder what all that's about?"

"We can only turn up and find out, I suppose," said Arty. "No use worrying about it in the meantime. I can't see what they can do to us."

The next day they got scrubbed-up for the meeting. Helen looked smashing, as usual. She wore a green suit and red shoes and with her red hair, looked anything but a road-marker. Arty and Joe wore jackets and ties. They looked almost respectable.

They were met at the steps of the Court House by Cliff, who took them into a big office, filled with people. They were still bringing chairs in from other rooms and adding them to the circle. There was Sergeant Freeman, Constable Scott and Cliff James in one group. Next to them were the County Engineer and the Town Clerk. Then there was Foxy, and next to him were three men in suits, two of them with briefcases.

Sergeant Freeman introduced Helen, Joe and Arty to the three men in suits. One of them was a Ministry of Works engineer, one was a lawyer and the other was an Inspector of something. It was all very confusing to Arty, Joe and Helen, who were seated next to the police contingent.

The Inspector of something opened his briefcase and took out a paper, glanced at it, and fired the first shot.

"You three are facing some quite serious charges, do you realise that?"

"We didn't think it was all that serious, sir," said Arty.

"Serious enough to have your vehicle confiscated and yourselves fined, or even imprisoned. It all depends on how cooperative you're prepared to be."

"We're cooperative, sir," said Arty.

"You've been finding gold in the roads around here, haven't you?"

"Some, sir, yes," said Arty.

"We want to know exactly how much gold you've found and where you found it," said the Inspector of something.

Arty and Joe and Helen looked at each other. Joe nodded and Helen shrugged.

"It's hard to say exactly, sir," said Arty. "They get the roading material from gold-bearing rivers and spread it out on the roads. The gold seems to be in patches, you could find some almost anywhere around here."

"Exactly how much gold have you been getting?"

said the Inspector.

"We've been averaging about five ounces a week, sir."

"For how long?"

"Six months."

"And how much an ounce do you get for it?"

"Five hundred dollars."

"That's a hundred and twenty ounces," said the lawyer, speaking for the first time. "Sixty thousand dollars' worth."

There was a short silence while everyone, except Arty and Joe and Helen, looked around at each other.

"Would you give us a few moments please?" said the Inspector to Arty, Joe and Helen, and Cliff got up and ushered them out of the room. They stood in the passage.

"What the hell's all that about?" said Joe.

"Don't ask me," said Arty. "I can't figure it out at all."

"You'd think we'd sold national secrets, or something," said Joe.

"Maybe we shouldn't have told them how much gold we got," said Helen. "It seemed to bother them."

"It wouldn't have made any difference," said Arty. "They'd find out easy enough if they wanted to. We haven't covered our tracks in that department very well. These blokes are serious. We'd better go along with them, and see what they've got up their sleeves."

After about ten minutes Cliff opened the door and waved them back into the room. They sat down again.

"Thank you," said the Inspector. "Now we need to know how many of you know about this gold in the roads."

"Us three and my wife," said Arty.

"No one else?"

"No, sir."

The Inspector paused for a few moments, and then he said, "Do you realise what would happen if it became publicly known that there's gold in this quantity in the roads around here?"

"You'd get people running all over the place with detectors," said Arty. "Diggin' up the roads and leaving holes everywhere. That's why we've been keeping it to ourselves."

"Yes," said the Inspector. "We'll take a lunch break now. Would you like to meet us back here at one-thirty?"

"Yes, sir," said Arty.

"And in the meantime we'd appreciate it if you wouldn't mention any of this to anyone else."

"Yes, sir."

The rest of them all went up to the pub for lunch. Arty, Joe and Helen ate in the tearooms.

"There's something going on here," said Arty. "Those blokes are worried about people finding out about the gold in the roads. They're not so worried about us. We might have them over a barrel."

"How do you make that out?" said Joe.

"We're in a position to start a gold rush on their roads, and they sure as hell don't want that. There'd be a hell of a mess. We'll just go along with them and see what they come up with."

They reassembled in the Court House office at one-thirty and the Inspector kicked off the proceedings.

"We don't want that gold in the roads," he said bluntly.

"There's none where we've been, sir," said Arty.

"How much road would you say you've cleared of gold in the six months you've been doing it?"

Arty and Joe looked to Helen.

"About three hundred kilometres," she said. "There's roughly twelve hundred kilometres we haven't done."

"Well we've decided to remove the gold from the roads in much the same way as you've been doing it. We've decided not to bring charges against you, providing you undertake to keep this whole matter confidential."

"Thank you, sir," said Arty, "but if you don't mind me saying so, I don't think you'd get away with it."

"Why not?"

"Well it takes weeks to learn how to operate a metal detector properly. They'd miss half of it at first. There's a special knack in interpreting the signal-responses that you can't just pick up like that."

"What would you suggest then?" said the Inspector.

"Why not let us do it?" said Arty. "We're all set-up for it. If you were to start training staff to recover gold from the roads it'd be public knowledge in no time. People can't keep quiet about a thing like that, sir. It'd start a gold-rush on the roads!"

"Yes, we've considered that," said the Inspector. "How long do you think it would take you to remove the gold from the remaining gold-bearing roads?"

"Full-time? Less than a year," said Arty. "Say a year at the outside."

"Very well," said the Inspector. "We'll consult about it and let you know what we decide. In the meantime we would ask you to respect the confidentiality of the matter."

"We're not going to blow the whistle on ourselves, sir," pointed out Arty.

"Yes, well, we'll be in touch with you within a few days. Thank you."

Cliff ushered Arty, Joe and Helen out. They got into the ute and picked up a dozen of beer from the pub and went round to Arty's place.

"I think we've got them," said Arty. "They can't prosecute us without letting the public know about the gold in the roads, and the only way they can be sure we'll keep quiet about it is to give us the job."

"I hope you're right," said Joe, who'd been opening mail. "We've missed out on the Southern Highway job. The

County's doing it themselves."

A week after that Arty, Joe and Helen were invited to a meeting at the Council Chambers. The Inspector, the Sergeant, the County Engineer, Foxy and Cliff James were there. For some reason they all shook hands, and then they sat at the big table in the Council Boardroom. The Inspector played around with papers.

"It has been decided to accept your offer to remove the gold from all the roads in this area, the situation to be reviewed on a monthly basis."

"Thank you, sir," said Arty. "We'll get the job done."

"I hope so. Now there'll be no payment for this work. You can keep whatever gold you happen to find. You'll be required to furnish Mr Bremner with details of what areas have been cleared of gold. No more gold-bearing roading material will be used, and Mr Bremner will advise you what areas contain that material."

"It's going to take a while to go back through the records and find what materials were taken from where," said the engineer.

"We've got plenty of road to go on with," said Helen. "I can let you have a map of what we've done and where we've found gold."

She'd already worked out that there was probably over two hundred thousand dollars' worth of gold left in the roads, going by what they'd already done.

"Thanks," said Bremner. He was going to be okay to work with.

"Officer Fox will cooperate and liaise with you on your progress," said the Inspector. "And I remind all of you again about the need for discretion and confidentiality in this matter."

They all agreed again on the need for discretion and

confidentiality and shook hands again and the meeting broke up.

The Sergeant held Arty and Joe and Helen up in the hallway to ask them if they knew anything about some rotten mussels that someone had placed inside the driver's door of Foxy's patrol car, and when they got outside The Fox himself was waiting by their ute.

"I don't want you lot to go imagining that you're going to get away with anything over this," he said. "I'll still be keeping an eye on you, and I'll be expecting you to keep within the regulations."

"No, Foxy," said Arty. "You're supposed to be cooperating with us, remember?"

"We'll see about that," said Foxy, and he stalked off towards his car.

"He never gives up, that bloke," said Joe.

"I almost feel sorry for him," said Helen.

"He's done us a favour in a way," said Arty.

"A favour? Foxy?"

"If it hadn't been for him hounding us and catching us we wouldn't have got the job. I hope he's there when we tell them they've got to dig up a hundred yards of the Boulder Creek Road. We'll save that until the last."

It was much easier now that they didn't have to do all that Foxy-dodging. They worked out a plan with the engineer and began to methodically prospect the roads of Matea, covering parts that had previously been too risky and working outwards from the town. The big bleep down by the County Depot gates turned out to be a ball of silver paper, and the two between Arty and Joe's place were pieces of gold.

Like all miners, they had their good days and bad days, but on the average they were getting between five and seven ounces of gold a week. No one questioned why a road-marking truck was being used for maintenance work on the roads, and

Foxy was no longer a threat, for the meantime. He still drove past a fair bit but he wasn't stopping these days, he was waiting.

Then one day when they were scanning a not-very-productive stretch of the Southern Highway two men in a plain car started following along behind them, openly watching them.

"I wonder what they want?" said Joe, squinting in his rear-vision mirror.

"Depends who they are," said Arty. "I don't like the look of this. We'd better suspend operations."

They pulled into a layby and stopped. The car stopped behind them and the two men came round to the road-marking truck and introduced themselves. They were Mines Department Inspectors. They started asking questions about what they were doing. It sounded like they'd seen them digging and filling in holes in the road.

Arty gave them the one about maintenance and cat's-eyes and reflector posts, and showed them the drum of rubbish on the truck.

"Some of this stuff works its way up through the seal," he explained, holding up a rusted piece of iron. "It could rip somebody's tyre to bits."

The Mines Department Inspectors didn't seem impressed.

"We're not satisfied that your operation complies with Mines Department regulations," said one of them.

"What's the Mines Department got to do with us?" said Arty. "We're road-markers!"

"You're retrieving material from beneath the surface of public ground, and that constitutes mining within the meaning of the act. Mining without a licence is quite a serious offence, you know. We'll just take your names and the address of your company, if you don't mind. We'll probably be in touch with you."

"They know something!" said Arty when the inspectors

were gone. "Someone's dobbed us in!"

"The Fox!" said Helen.

"The bastard!" said Joe.

"It could have been him all right," said Arty.

"It must have been him," said Helen. "They even talked like him."

"What would he have to gain by putting our pot on?" said Joe.

"I don't know," said Arty. "It's hard to tell how Foxy's mind works. It might have something to do with us dropping that tree on his patrol car that time. We can't even be sure it's him. I think we'd better go and see the Sarge about this. It might get serious."

They found Sergeant Freeman in his office and Arty explained to him what had happened.

"Damn it, Arty!" said the Sergeant. "This gold-in-the-roads thing you've started has been nothing but a bloody nuisance!"

"It's not us, Sarge," protested Arty. "We're doin' a good job out there. The nuisance is whoever blew the whistle on us!"

"It's Foxy!" said Helen.

"He's always pickin' on us," said Joe. "It's him all right!"

"Where's your proof of that?" said the Sergeant.

"We haven't got any proof, Sarge," said Arty. "But it has to be him. He's the only one with an axe to grind."

"You can't make accusations without proof," said the Sergeant. "I'll get in touch with Inspector Bradford and tell him what's going on. In the meantime you'd better keep that outfit of yours off the road. I'll let you know what they decide."

They decided on another meeting in the Council Chambers. The Inspector of Something was there with his lawyer, one of the Mines Department Inspectors and another bloke were there, Don Bremner was there, and the Sergeant and Cliff James were there. The Fox was there too, looking far too nonchalant to be anything but guilty, as far as Arty, Joe and Helen were concerned. They all sat around the big table in the Council Boardroom.

"There's been a serious breach of security in your clearing of gold from the roads in this region," said the Inspector of Something to Arty, Joe and Helen. "You know that it's a condition of the – er – operation that strict confidentiality be maintained at all times."

"Don't worry about us, sir," said Arty, looking directly at Foxy. "We haven't let on anything to anyone about anything."

"How much of the road has been cleared of gold at this point, Mr Bremner?"

"Eight hundred and thirty Ks," said Bob, consulting a paper. "We've got approximately four hundred and twenty Ks that could still contain gold."

"I want to stress with you again the need for security in this matter," said the Inspector, looking around the room at all of them. "If it becomes publicly known about this gold in the roads we'll have a dangerous and chaotic situation on our hands."

The inspector shuffled papers for a few moments, and then he went on, "We've been contacted by Mr Drew here of the Mines Department, and it appears that there are certain formalities that have been overlooked. Mr Drew's department is prepared to co-operate with us for the duration of this – er – exercise. Mr Drew has prepared the necessary documents for you, Mr Brown. They can be witnessed on behalf of the Transport Department by Officer Fox."

After another reminder of the need for security the meeting broke up. The Mines Inspector and Arty and Foxy went into Bob Bremner's office and signed and witnessed a number of forms, and Arty met Joe and Helen out on the footpath with a Prospecting Licence on a specified four hundred and twenty Ks of county roads with a special clause about restoring the surface to its original condition wherever it was disturbed. Signed by Foxy himself.

The word 'disturbed' tickled their fancy and they ended up calling a place where they'd dug up the road to get a piece of gold 'a disturbance'. They'd set off in the mornings to do a bit of 'surface-disturbing'.

"We could put down our occupation as 'Disturbers of the Surface'!" laughed Helen.

Joe was 'The Scanner of the Surface', Arty became 'The Disturber of the Surface' (a title for him that Foxy himself would have approved of), and Helen was 'The Restorer of the Surface'. They referred to each other as The Scanner, The Disturber or The Restorer. It was a bit of humour amongst them and fitted in with the undercover aspects of the operation.

"We've got three hundred and seventy Ks to go," said Helen one day, bending over a marked-off road map on Arty and Carol's new kitchen table. "That's not counting the Boulder Creek deposit."

"How long do you reckon that's going to take us, Honey?" said Joe.

"It depends on how many times we have to stop," she said. "Roughly two months, taking it on average."

"It's getting round to time for us to tell Bob Bremner he's got to dig up a hundred yards of the Boulder Creek Road and stick it through a screening plant for us," said Arty.

"Wonder how he'll take that?" said Joe.

"He won't like it," predicted Arty, and he was right.

"Out of the question!" said Bob. "I couldn't authorise a thing like that! I couldn't possibly justify the cost of it!"

"It'll cost you more than that if people find out how much gold there is in that bit of road," said Arty. "They'd dismantle it for you! It's not going to cost you much anyway. All you have to provide is a digger and a grader and a roller for a couple of days. We can cut it down to single lane and put the top two feet through a screening plant and straight back onto the road. It's a piece of cake, Bob!"

"It might be for you," said Bob. "But I don't know. I'll have to think about it."

By the time they'd finished the last few Ks of gold-bearing road and prodded him a few times, Bob Bremner was resigned to digging up the Boulder Creek Deposit and putting it through a gold-screening plant they'd borrowed. It took four days and they took eighteen ounces of gold out of the hundred yards of road. Nine thousand dollars' worth. A triumphant finale to Arty Brown's only successful undertaking in living memory!

Helen informed them that they'd taken 587 ounces of gold out of the roads in Matea County, and in spite of them having spent up large on their gold-selling trips to Danby there was $248,000 in the Southern Road-marking account.

"I always knew we'd crack it one day," said Arty, contentedly pouring home brew into his glass and overflowing it with froth.

"Here's to our next little enterprise, whatever that might be!"

"Oh no!" said Carol.

"Don't worry, dear," said Arty. "We'll be okay now we've got a bit of capital behind us. It takes money to make money you know."

"I wouldn't know," said Carol. "We've never had any money before. I just wonder how long it's going to last."

BAR

Eight Thousand Bottles and a Dog

IT LASTED for six months, a rather interesting and eventful six months, as it turned out.

Two hundred and forty-eight thousand dollars sounds like a lot of money, but it's not that hard to go through a lot of money when you've never had a lot of money before. Firstly there was the tax on it, which Helen insisted they pay before they started spending any. That took $82,700 off it, leaving $166,300 to divide between the two families, $83,150 each. And once they'd got that sorted out they set about spending some of it.

The kids had to have new bikes, and a computer for their education. A new ute for Joe and Helen. A new car for Carol. Arty made her get a flash one with all the optional extras. Joe and Helen had a double garage built, with a door leading straight into the house. Arty and Carol had their house painted.

On a trip to Danby they all got carried away and went on a spending spree and came home with the new ute piled high with new appliances of every description, from food-processors to cellphones.

It wasn't all plain sailing for Arty, modern gear got him flustered. For example, there was a digital watch he bought himself. They'd set it on the right time and date for him at the shop where he bought it, but he pushed a couple of the buttons, just to see, and finished up with it flashing hopelessly out of time, the date wrong and in French, and an alarm that kept going off. Very disconcerting, especially when you're talking to someone. He took it off and stuck it in his pocket, but it still kept going off all the time. He ended up giving the thing to his nine-year-old boy, who had it adjusted properly in no time, and commandeered it for his trouble.

It was the same with the new television set and video player. They operated on remote control and Arty never mastered more than the on-off and channel-changing functions. Carol was fully extended getting the hang of the new washing machine and microwave oven, and if Arty wanted to watch a video or record a programme he had to get his kids to set it up for him. The cellphone remained a funny name to Arty.

The new radio and compact-disc player was another mystery that Arty gave up trying to solve, and he nearly pranged Carol's new car trying to get the electric windows to go up. It was an automatic and Arty didn't like them. He missed his clutch and gear-lever, so he got Joe to run him over to Danby, where he bought himself a second-hand three-ton truck, a diesel one. He was happy with that and drove it everywhere, even though he had nothing useful to do with it.

Helen, on the other hand, liked Carol's new car. She liked it so much that she had to have one of her own, a red one, and she looked real snazzy getting around in it with her long red hair.

Then Arty went and bought himself a dog. A brindle one. It was a racing greyhound called High Roller. He got it off a bloke he knew who bred them on the other side of town, and paid $2750 for it. He turned up at Joe's place with it in the cab of his truck and dragged it out on its lead.

"It's a very well-bred dog this, Joe. Just ready to start racing. There's big money in it if you can get onto a winner."

"What if you don't?" said Joe, reaching down to pat

the cringing, shivering dog.

"Don't what?"

"Get onto a winner? What if it can't run fast enough?"

"It'll run all right," said Arty. "Both its father and mother have won a lot of money. And I can still get my money back on it for breeding. It'll probably turn out to be a champion!"

"It doesn't look like a champion to me," said Joe.

"You can't tell yet," said Arty. "It'll have to be trained up. I've got all the info on how to go about it. I'll have him racing in about a month."

High Roller was housed, or kennelled, in the cab of an old truck down in Arty's yard. He had to have two kgs of prime steak and a lot of vitamins and other stuff every day. He had to be taken for walks and runs and no one but Arty was allowed to feed him, exercise him, or even pat him. He was a professional racing dog, in training. Carol thought the dog was harmless enough, it was keeping Arty out of mischief, but she didn't know how much he'd paid for it and what he was feeding it on.

In spite of all the attention and tucker that was being lavished on him, High Roller still had an air of misery about him. Even Arty had to admit it when Joe pointed out that the dog didn't appear to be settling down. Arty decided to consult the local vet about it. The vet diagnosed that the dog was suffering from several different species of intestinal worms, and charged Arty nearly a hundred dollars for dosing him, which, a week later, had made no visible difference to High Roller's appearance or demeanour. He was as lugubrious as ever.

"It still looks like a useless blimmin' mongrel of a thing to me," said Joe to Helen. "I hope Arty knows what he's doing."

"It can't do any harm," replied Helen. "At least it's

keeping Arty out of trouble."

Finally Arty pronounced that High Roller was ready to race. On the Sunday of the dog races up in Danby they set off for the big occasion, the launching of High Roller's racing career. Helen, Carol and the kids travelled in Carol's car, and Arty and Joe followed in the ute, with the dog in a specially-made wooden crate on the back.

At the track Arty put his dog in a cage behind the starting gate and stayed with it right up until the race started, in case it got nervous. It was a six-dog race. The dogs were put in the starting stalls, the hare was set off along the rail and the starter opened the gates. Five dogs dived off up the track after the hare. High Roller loped off after them losing ground at every stride. He evidently hadn't seen the hare, or if he had he must have instinctively known that he was never going to be able to catch up with it, because he wasn't trying. He followed the pack as far as the first bend, then he stopped, looked around, trotted across to the rail and cocked his leg on a post and scratched at the ground. A big roar of laughter went up from the crowd.

Arty was embarrassed, and embarrassed some more when the dog wouldn't let him catch it. He chased it around on the course trying to get its lead on it, but it kept dodging away from him. The race was over. The commentator was commentating on Arty's efforts to capture High Roller, and the crowd was enjoying it immensely.

The dog finally got through the fence and among the crowd. They cornered it in the doorway of a building and Arty got its lead on and led it away, to the accompaniment of loud cheering and clapping.

High Roller was entered in two other races that day but Arty decided that the safest thing to do was scratch him. He was put in his crate on the ute and they headed back to Matea.

They'd been at the race track for just under an hour. Carol and Helen and the kids had already left, in case anyone thought they had anything to do with Arty and Joe and High Roller.

"I'm getting rid of this blasted dog," said Arty. "I'm not going through that again, it's too embarrassing."

"We could take it out into the country somewhere and then run away and leave it behind," joked Joe.

"The bloke I got him off said I could take him back if I wasn't satisfied with him," said Arty. "He's going back, I'm going to get as much of my money back as I can."

Arty didn't only lose face over High Roller, he lost a considerable amount of money as well. All the bloke would refund him was $350, on the grounds that Arty seemed to have badly mistrained the dog and hadn't given it a fair trial. A loss of $2,500.

"Sometimes a man's got to cut his losses and get on with life," said Arty philosophically. "You can't let a dog run your life like that. I'd rather have a horse, a race horse."

"No!" said Carol. "No more animals."

"I'll second that," said Helen.

"A man's got to do something," said Arty. "You can't go giving up just because you have a bit of a set-back."

"I wish you would give up," sighed Carol. "The safest thing you could do would be nothing."

"Don't worry, dear," said Arty cheerfully. "You just wait. One of these days me and Joe are going to hit the jackpot."

"That would make a nice change from being a crackpot," laughed Carol.

Arty and Joe had nothing to do, which can be harder to handle than too much to do. Now that they could afford to spend time in the pub it wasn't so much fun any more.

They were sitting in Arty's truck watching the traffic go past.

"I've been thinking, Joe," said Arty.

"What about this time?" said Joe with some apprehension.

"The Prof. We owe him, you know. If it wasn't for him we'd never have been able to find that gold in the first place. I'd like to do something for him, or give him something."

"Me too," agreed Joe. "What does he need, I wonder?"

"He doesn't seem to need money. He's only interested in the booze, and it's no good giving him too much of that."

"Why don't we give him the Boulder Creek Nugget?" suggested Joe.

They'd kept some of the best nuggets they'd found and the one they'd got out of the Boulder Creek Deposit was a particularly beautiful one. Over half an ounce and heart-shaped, rounded and rolled, with a small natural hole through it. It was by far the prettiest piece of gold they'd found with the gold-bar the Prof had made for them.

"That's a great idea!" said Arty enthusiastically. "Let's do that. We'll have to tell Helen and Carol first though."

"Why?"

"Well for one thing Helen's got the nuggets stashed away somewhere, and we're going to have to explain where it went anyway."

Helen and Carol agreed to part with the Boulder Creek Nugget when they told them what they wanted to do with it, and the next day Arty and Joe took it round to The Prof's place, wrapped in a piece of white tissue paper in a matchbox. As they picked their way round the side of The Prof's house they could see exactly what The Prof needed most.

"We could get rid of all these bottles for him," said Arty. "We've got the truck for it."

"Sure needs it," agreed Joe, sweeping a stray bottle off the footpath with his foot. "Let's offer to do that for him."

They found The Prof exactly as they'd last seen him, bleary and vague and unkempt and surrounded by empty wine bottles and papers and magazines. He greeted them politely and invited them into his smelly, over-heated kitchen. They shifted empty bottles out of the way and sat at the table.

"What can I do for you?" enquired The Prof, pouring himself a wee nip and sitting down.

"We've got something for you, Prof," said Arty, passing him the matchbox across the bottle-cluttered table. "It's an appreciation for making the gold-bar for us."

The Prof opened the matchbox and peered at the Boulder Creek Nugget, lying ancient and gleaming and mysterious on its bed of tissue paper.

"It's the best piece of gold we found," said Joe. "We reckon you ought to have it."

"My goodness," said The Prof. "It is rather beautiful, isn't it? But I can't accept this," he added, looking up.

"Why not? You earned it," said Arty.

"It's got a hole in it," said The Prof, and he chuckled his chuckle and poured himself another wee nip and quaffed a hefty slug of it. "You didn't have to do this," he added, peering again at the nugget.

"We want you to have it," said Arty. "We owe you that."

"That's very nice of you, I must say," said the Prof. "It is rather beautiful," he said again. "I thank you both."

"How would you like us to cart a few of these empty bottles away for you, Prof?" said Joe. "We've bought ourselves a truck and we've got nothing to do at the moment."

"I've been wondering what to do about the bottles," said The Prof vaguely. "They won't take them back, you know. I'm afraid they've been accumulating."

"We can get rid of them no trouble at all," said Arty.

"That would be a great favour," said The Prof. "I don't know what to say."

"Don't say anything," said Arty. "Leave it to us. We'll take a load of them this afternoon."

After lunch they backed the truck down the side of The Prof's house and started loading bottles onto it. The Prof was down at the pub. They cleared his kitchen first, putting the bottles into cartons and emptying them out onto the truck. Joe dragged open the door into the passage.

"Bloody hell, Arty!" he said. "You'd better come and have a look at this!"

"Bloody hell," echoed Arty, looking into the passage.

The whole passage was filled with empty bottles, with a narrow path up the middle of it.

"I wonder what it's like in those rooms?" said Joe.

"I'm scared to look," said Arty. "If we can get the front door open we can back the truck up to the veranda and fire the bottles straight onto it."

The bedrooms off the passage were free of bottles and full of dusty, dilapidated, cheap furniture. They hadn't been used or even opened up for years. By the time they'd cleared all the bottles out of the house and from around the back door they had a full load of them.

On their way to the tip they passed The Prof, tottering along home with his couple of bottles of wine in a plastic bag. They tooted the horn and waved out to him but he didn't see or hear them.

At the tip there was a concrete bay set aside for bottles. They backed up to it and raised the hoist and tipped two tons of bottles into it in a great crashing cascade that overflowed the sides, back and front of the bay. The tip manager came running over.

"What the hell are you doing?" he shouted.

"A few bottles for you, Pete," said Arty cheerfully. "We've got another load or two for you yet."

"Like hell you have. The bay's more than full already."

"What do you expect us to do with them then?" said Arty. "This is only half of them."

"You're not bringing any more of them here," said Pete. "We can't handle that many bottles at once."

"Well why don't we stick 'em straight over the tip-face?" said Arty.

"Not allowed to," said Pete. "All the bottles have to go into the glass bay to be recycled. They only clear it once a month."

"When's it going to be cleared next?"

"I don't know, two or three weeks. In the meantime I'm not taking any more bottles."

"What are we supposed to do with them?"

"I don't care what you do with the bloody things, but you're not bringing any more of them here until the bay's cleared. I haven't got room for any more, and that's that. Now shift your truck, I want to get the tractor past."

Arty and Joe drove off.

"What are we going to do about that?" said Joe. "We've got at least another load to get rid of."

"We'll think of something," said Arty. "We'll load 'em on and then worry about what we're going to do with them after that."

The next morning they returned to The Prof's place and cleaned up the rest of his bottles. It made a very full load but they got them all on the truck. The Prof emerged and tried to help, but only succeeded in getting in the way. When they'd finished, The Prof's house and yard looked quite naked. He hadn't seen it like that for years.

"I'm very grateful to you chaps," he said.

"Don't mention it, Prof," said Arty. "Not a problem."

But the problems were coming up. For a start there was the problem of what to do with this huge load of bottles.

"We'll have to leave 'em on the truck until we work out what we're going to do with them," said Arty.

"We could hire a digger and dig a hole and bury them," said Joe.

"Where?" said Arty.

"Good question," said Joe.

"Something'll crop up," said Arty.

Something did. It was Carol. When she got home and saw the truck piled high with empty wine bottles parked there she cropped up good and properly.

"What are all those bottles on the truck?" she said in her schoolteacher voice.

"Nothing, dear," said Arty. "It's just some bottles we're cleaning up for The Prof. It's a favour we're doing for him."

"What are you going to do with them?"

"They were supposed to go to the tip but they can't take them at the moment. We're just hanging onto them until we can work out how to get rid of them."

"You're not hanging onto them here," said Carol. "I won't have it. You can take them somewhere else, right now."

"Aw, come on, dear. We've got nowhere to take them to."

"Right now," said Carol. "I mean it!"

She meant it. Arty drove the truck round to Joe's place.

"You'd better follow me in the ute, Joe. Carol won't let us park the truck at home with these bottles on it. If we leave it on the street Foxy'll slap a ticket on it for sure. We'll have to find somewhere to put it for the meantime."

They drove around trying to find somewhere to park their truckload of bottles, and as they passed Foxy's house Arty noticed that the vacant section next to Foxy's place was still for sale, had been for months, and that gave him an idea. He drove in and parked on the section, right alongside Foxy's house. Foxy wasn't there.

"What are you doing?" said Joe. "You'll get us in trouble with Foxy, parking here like this!"

"No, I don't think so," said Arty. "I've got an idea how we can get Foxy to look after this for us. It's about time he did something useful for somebody."

"Oh no!" said Joe.

"Don't worry," said Arty. "I've got it all worked out. Give us a hand here."

He explained his plan as they got out a tool-kit and unbolted the fuel pump off the motor of the truck. They put the pump on the floor of Joe's ute, locked up the truck, and went down town to the real estate agent's office, where they bought a month's option on the section for $150. The full price of it was $18,500. Then they called in at the pub for a beer on the way home.

"I don't think Foxy's going to like this," said Joe.

"There's nothing he can do about us parking our own truck on our own place," said Arty. "We'll probably lose our hundred and fifty bucks, but it'll be worth it just to see what Foxy does about it."

They'd just got out of the ute at Arty's place when there was a squeal of tyres as Foxy's prowl car turned into the street. He pulled up beside them with a skid and got out of the car looking almost emotional.

"What do you think you're playing at, Arty?" he demanded.

"What do you mean, Foxy?" said Arty innocently.

"What's your truck doing parked at my place with all those filthy booze bottles on it?"

"That's not your place," said Arty, "it's our place. We've bought an option on it. I can show you the papers if you like. Here they are here."

He reached in and took the option papers out of the glovebox of the ute and handed them to Foxy, who glanced at them and shoved them back to him.

"You're not leaving that load of bottles next to my fence. I'm ordering you to remove it immediately."

"Sorry, Foxy. We couldn't do that, even if we wanted to. The truck's broken down. The fuel pump's packed a sad on us, we've got it here, look," and he opened the door and showed Foxy the pump on the floor of the ute. "I'm afraid it'll have to stay there until we can get this up to Danby to be overhauled."

Foxy was speechless with rage.

"We'll have to get you to keep an eye on our truck for us until we can get it running again," went on Arty. "Seeing as we're going to be neighbours we might as well get off on the right foot, cooperating with each other and all that."

"You can't get away with that," snarled Foxy. "I'll complain!"

"You're pretty good at that," said Arty, "but you can't tell anyone what to do with their own vehicle on their own place. Not even you."

"I'm going to get you for this," snarled Foxy. "You've gone too far this time."

"We've heard that somewhere before," said Arty. "Now if you've got no more business to discuss, we're fairly busy . . ."

"I'll get you for this," repeated Foxy, getting into his car and slamming the door.

"Don't forget your seat-belt," said Arty, as Foxy began to take off without putting it on. "There's a law against that sort of thing around here."

"That's about the best value I ever had for a hundred and fifty bucks," grinned Arty, as they watched Foxy disappear round the corner.

Three weeks after that the contractor got them to take the load of bottles up to the recycling plant in Danby, to save double-handling it, for which they charged him a hundred and fifty dollars.

"I like the idea of putting one across on The Fox," said Arty with satisfaction as they returned to Matea. "It makes him seem almost human."

"If he ever gets a chance to nail us he'll do it now," said Joe.

"He would have anyway," said Arty. "I'm afraid Foxy was standing behind the door when the milk of human kindness was being handed out."

One day Foxy pulled Helen up and gave her a ticket for doing sixty Ks in a 50-K zone, and by the time they'd paid the fine they discovered that they had less than fifteen hundred dollars left in the bank and bills to pay. By this time Arty and Carol had gone through all their money and were back to living on Carol's wages.

"Well that's a beaut!" said Arty, sitting with Joe in the cab of the truck. "It's hard to believe we could have gone through all that money so quick."

"Helen reckons we spent a hundred and thirty thousand of it on vehicles," said Joe. "We've still got those."

"Yeah," said Arty, "and they all cost money to run, and that's what we've just run out of."

"There's road-marking coming up on Highway 81 next month," said Joe. "We'll probably get that."

"Yeah, I was talking to Bob about it the other day," said Arty. "But we need something to tide us over, we've got some bills that need payin'."

"Us too," said Joe. "Helen's talking of selling her car."

"We ought to try and avoid that," said Arty. "Helen worked as hard getting that gold as any of us, she deserves to have a decent car out of it. I'd rather sell this truck if it came to that."

"But the truck could be our way of making a living," said Joe. "All we need is some work for it."

"That's the tricky bit," said Arty. "We're going to have to start selling stuff if something doesn't turn up by the end of the week."

But he didn't have to wait that long. They drove round to Joe's place to drop him off and when they got there Helen had good news. A reprieve. She'd just had a phone call. The new owners of the Matea Timber Yard had offered her back her old job in the office, with a small pay rise.

"Did you accept it?" said Joe.

"Of course I did," she said. "I start on Monday."

"Well that's the weight off us for the moment," said Joe.

"Good on you!" said Arty.

And the next day Arty got a reprieve of his own. He rang Joe with the good news.

"I've sold a whole lot of the stuff out of my shed," he said.

"How come?" said Joe. "Who'd want any of that?"

"A crowd from Danby called Visuals Limited. They're coming back for another van-load tomorrow. They made me an offer for a lot of the stuff in the shed and quite a few of the things I've got outside as well. It doesn't even have to work, they only want it for props."

"Who are they?" said Joe.

"Someone put them onto me. They specialise in dressing up sets for films and telly ads and they're keen to get hold of anything that's a bit dated. I knew that stuff of mine was going to become valuable one of these days. They've just about cleaned out me shed," he added, though you couldn't, in fact, see where it had been taken from.

"How much did you get for it?" said Joe.

"Thirteen hundred bucks, and they're coming back for more!"

"Well that's a relief," said Joe. "We're off the hook for the time being. Saved by the shed, eh!"

So they were back where they were in the good old chickens-and-cabbages days, except that their vehicles were updated.

"We'll get a break one of these days," said Arty philosophically. "All we have to do is wait for the opportunity and strike while the iron's hot!"

"Yes, dear," sighed Carol.

PAT TREMBETH

MOSSLE

The Jackpot

"We don't seem to be getting anywhere," said Arty. "I've been trying to work out where we've been going wrong." He and Joe were sitting in the ute out at the tip, where they'd been given a day's work gathering up rubbish that had been blown against the fences.

"I still blame The Fox for a lot of it," said Joe. "He's interfered with everything we've tried to do."

"Yeah, but Foxy's a fact of life around here now. I hear he's even bought that house he's living in. We just have to learn to live with him. No, a lot of it's our own fault when you look at it."

"How do you make that out?"

"Well, look at those chickens we reared that time. We'd have been all right if we'd only fenced them in. And we'd have done all right out of those cabbages if we'd only spread 'em out a bit. And we'd still have our rubbish-collection job if we'd had the truck insured. We've got to take a bit of responsibility for that. And dropping that tree on Foxy's car – that was his fault that time and we got the blame for it. And blowing up the pub lavatory – we can't blame them for blaming us for that. And there's all that carry-on out at Merv's pub, you have to admit it was us who caused that."

"We did all right out of the gold in the roads," Joe reminded him.

"Even that had its problems we could have avoided if

we'd used our heads," said Arty. "I've been thinking."

"Oh no!" said Joe.

"No," said Arty. "What we've been doing is trying to crack it for big money all at once, and we're just not cut out for big money. It's no good for us. What we need is steady, permanent work to keep us occupied and bring in a reasonable living."

"I wouldn't argue with that," said Joe. "But what?"

"Well the road-marking we get is about half what we need to make wages and keep our heads above water. We just need something else to supplement it. If we aim for that rather than trying to make it big we might find something that works. These one-off jobs are no good to us."

"It doesn't look to me as though we've got that much choice," said Joe. "We still have to take whatever comes up."

"Yeah, but I'll only feel all right when we get some kind of steady permanent work that keeps us going full-time. I hate having to ask Helen for money all the time. It's . . ."

"Look out!" said Joe. "Here comes The Fox!"

They saw Foxy's prowl car turn into the tip gate.

"He's coming over here," said Arty.

"We haven't done anything lately, have we?" said Joe.

"Not that I know of," said Arty. "But you never know with Foxy."

Foxy pulled up behind the ute and came round to the cab. They saw with horror that he was trying to smile. To Arty and Joe it was a hideous and ominous sight.

"What do you want now, Foxy?" said Arty uncomfortably.

"I've just been talking to Helen," said Foxy. "She said I'd find you two out here."

"What's wrong now?" said Joe.

"There's nothing wrong," said Foxy. "I've been asked

to put a proposition to you."

"What sort of a proposition?" said Arty.

"I'm not at liberty to say at this stage," said Foxy officiously, "but if you'd like to attend a meeting at the County Engineer's office at nine-thirty tomorrow morning we'll be able to tell you more about it."

"Who's we?" said Joe.

"You'll find out at the meeting," said Foxy, trying to smile again and producing an unaccustomed grimace. "But I think you'll find it's to your advantage."

He tried to smile again and when he got no smile in return he mumbled something about "See you at the meeting" and left.

"What's all that about, I wonder?" said Arty.

"He was trying to be nice," said Joe incredulously.

"Yeah, and he's not very good at it, is he?" said Arty. "There's something going on, that's for sure."

"Something to our advantage, he reckons."

"We'll have to wait and see about that," said Arty. "I can't imagine The Fox doing anything to anyone's advantage. There's got to be a catch in it somewhere. It'll be interesting to hear what he's got to say at this meeting. It looks to me as though he's been told to keep on the right side of us over something."

Bob Bremner seemed pleased to see them when they arrived at his office the next morning. He said "Thanks for coming," and ushered them into his office and sat them down. Foxy was already there and, horrors, he tried to smile again.

"I'll get straight to the point," said Bob. "You blokes are in a position to help us out."

"How's that?" said Arty.

"We've been authorised to proceed with re-sealing State Highway 81," said Bob.

"That's good news. We'll mark it for you, if that's what you want."

"There's a slight problem that'll have to be sorted out before we can start," said Bob. "When we put in our estimate for the job it was based on us being able to take our material from the Turnbull riverbed, but since you blokes found that gold in the roads we've been instructed not to take any more material from the Turnbull or any of its tributaries."

He stood up and went to a map on the wall and ran his finger across it. "We've been getting our metal from up here at Forks, from the Greycliff River. That's an extra forty-seven Ks we have to cart it, and we wouldn't be able to get enough from there anyway. The nearest other supply we know of is over here in the Pilson River, nearly sixty Ks from the job, and we'd have to put an access road in to it. That makes it impossible for us to do the job on the money we've been allocated for it."

"What's that got to do with us?" said Arty. "We haven't got any money."

"We've managed to get permission to use material from the Turnbull, providing we can guarantee there's no gold in it, and that's where you blokes come in. It wouldn't be economical for us to put all our material through a gold-plant, it'd slow the operation down too much, but if you could run your detectors over it once we've put it on the road, and remove any gold from it, that'd solve the problem for us. Would you be prepared to do that?"

"Yeah, I s'pose we could do that," said Arty noncommitally, "but we'd need a guarantee that we get all the marking and maintenance work on a permanent basis, otherwise it's not worth us keeping the unit on the road. It's costing us two thousand dollars a year just for the government inspection of our gear."

"I'm not in a position to guarantee that," said Bob. "It's not my department, but I can see that it's taken into consideration. The Department is anxious to make sure that the roads are free of gold. The nearest other road-markers operate out of Danby, you should be able to quote under them for any work in this County. That's all I can promise you, but we'll need all the material we take from the Turnbull scanned for gold. You can be reasonably sure of getting that work, and you do get to keep any gold you find. You should do all right out of it."

"There's another thing," said Arty.

"What's that?"

"Helen's not available to work with us any more. She's got a job. Gold removal is a three-man job. We'd need you to provide someone to move our signs around and direct the traffic for us. We couldn't afford to train anyone and pay their wages."

"We've been promised full co-operation from Foxy's Department," said Bob. "I'm sure he can take care of that for you, eh Foxy?"

Foxy wasn't trying to smile any more. He looked as though he was trying to swallow something too big for his throat.

"I could spare some time from my other duties," he said reluctantly.

"Your other duties'll be pleased to hear about that," said Arty.

"I won't be putting up with any nonsense," said Foxy petulantly. "It's all going to be done according to the law."

"According to Foxy, you mean," said Joe.

"All right," said Bob sharply. "That'll be enough of that, which reminds me of another thing. The Department is anxious that this thing about gold in the roading material doesn't become public knowledge. It's under investigation in two or three other places around the country. The fewer people who know about it in the meantime the better."

"Don't worry about us, Bob," said Arty. "We've never told anyone else about it yet and we're not likely to. If it does get out it won't be anything to do with us. It wouldn't be in our interests."

"Well that's settled then," said Bob. "We can go ahead and start stockpiling gravel out at Highway 81. I'll let you know when we're ready for you to start scanning it for us."

The meeting broke up, and Arty and Joe drove back out to the tip to finish off what they'd started the day before. They couldn't wait to tell the women about them having steady permanent work at last.

It was a bit hard for Helen and Carol to believe at first, especially when Arty and Joe told them that Foxy would be working with them.

"I always told you we'd hit the jackpot one of these days if we didn't give up trying," said Arty, spilling home brew froth on Carol's tablecloth.

"Yes dear," sighed Carol, still a bit sceptical.

And after all she'd put up with, sticking to Arty along the way, you could hardly blame her.

It turned out to be slow and not very productive work. They could scan the road a lot faster than the M.O.W. could re-seal it, and they weren't getting much gold. They were taking the roading material from a not-very-rich part of the river. Arty and Joe would let them finish a section and then go out and run the bar over it. Then they'd have to wait for another stretch to be finished. They were getting slightly better than wages from the gold they found.

Foxy wasn't needed, as it turned out. The traffic was already slowed down by the road works and it was easy to direct it around the road-marking unit. Foxy was stopping the traffic and letting several vehicles build up before waving them on, which was slowing everything down unnecessarily. Arty and Joe finally got hacked off with it.

"You might as well pack up and go home, Foxy," said Arty. "You're only getting in the road out here."

"What do you mean?" said Foxy. "Who's going to stop the traffic?"

"No one. It doesn't need stopping. They only need to be slowed down and kept moving. You're holding everyone up."

"Are you trying to tell me I don't know my job?" demanded Foxy.

"No, I'm trying to tell you we know ours, and you're confusing everything."

There was a squeal of tyres as a car came around the corner and had to brake hard to avoid colliding with cars held up by Foxy. Arty went out onto the road and waved the line of cars on.

"You see what I mean?" he said. "You're going to cause an accident if you keep backing the traffic up to the corners like that."

"You can't talk to me like that," said Foxy. "I'll have you know I'm in charge of this operation. I have to put in reports you know."

"Well why don't you just run along and put in a few reports, before you have an accident to report. We want to get on with the job."

"I've got more to do than hang around here doing your work for you," said Foxy petulantly. "I'm neglecting my other work to do this."

"Well don't let us hold you up," said Arty. "You're not needed here – come on, Joe, let's move this thing along."

Foxy hung around for a little while and then drove off in his prowl car. He didn't come back that day, in fact the next time they saw him to talk to was a real turn-up. It was about a week later, Arty and Joe were parked in a lay-by, sitting in the road-marking truck eating their lunch when The Fox pulled in behind them and came limping along.

"Something's up," whispered Joe. "He's trying to smile again."

"I thought I'd find you chaps out here," said Foxy in a rusty attempt at being friendly.

"What can we do for you Foxy?"

"I need a small favour," said Foxy. "I was wondering if you chaps would make a small purchase for me."

"What sort of a purchase?"

"I've got a list here," said Foxy, and he took a folded paper out of his top pocket. Arty reached out the truck window and took it from him and unfolded it.

"Two three-litre casks of white table wine and two dozen small bottles of beer," he read out. "What's this all about? Have you taken up secret drinking, Foxy?"

"Don't be ridiculous," said Foxy primly. "I wouldn't touch the filthy stuff. It's for a function I've been asked to organise."

"What sort of function?"

"It's the Annual Regional Convention of Traffic Officers. I've been asked to host it here in Matea."

"When's this supposed to come off?" said Joe.

"Next Friday night. I've already organised the hall and the caterers. All I need now is those drinks."

"Well why don't you go down to the pub and buy the stuff?" said Arty.

"I don't buy liquor," said Foxy indignantly. "It's only that I've been asked to provide a reasonable amount of the stuff and act as toastmaster. It would save me some embarrassment if you'd just purchase it for me, that's all."

"We can buy it for you," said Arty. "But how many are supposed to be there, half a dozen?"

"There are forty registered. I've already arranged their accommodation."

"Two casks of wine and two dozen stubbies among forty off-duty traffic cops? That wouldn't last half an hour."

"Don't you think it's going to be quite enough?"

"Nowhere near it," scoffed Arty. "You're a bit out of your depth here, Foxy. Who have you got for your drinks waiters?"

"Well, no one. I was going to set the drinks out on the tables and let them help themselves."

"What about glasses?"

"I've got paper cups."

"That's no good Foxy," said Arty. "You're only going to embarrass yourself, the way you're going. Who's paying for all this?"

"We've got a convention fund. I've kept expenses to a minimum."

"Well you're going to have to stock the bar in the hall and get someone to pour the drinks and serve them."

"I can't do that," protested Foxy. "I don't want anything to do with the filthy stuff."

"Tell you what we'll do for you, Foxy," said Arty. "We'll give you a price to supply the drinks and run the whole booze side of it for you. These things have to be done right or the whole thing'll be a flop."

"I want the liquor kept to an absolute minimum," said Foxy.

"We can do that for you. You can't control it if you just stick it out on the tables and let them hog into it. We'll personally serve the drinks and make sure no one overdoes it."

"Very well then," said Foxy. "I'll leave the liquor to you. You can let me know the cost, but remember to keep it to a minimum."

"Sure, Foxy. We can arrange it so we only pay for what gets used."

Foxy departed.

"This'll be a bit of humour," said Arty.

"Hell!" said Joe, awestruck by the thought. "Forty traffic cops in one heap!"

"Thirty-nine traffic cops and one Fox," Arty corrected him.

They got four casks of red wine and four of white, three fifty-litre kegs of beer, a bottle of whisky and one of gin, borrowed boxes of wine and beer glasses and some carafes from the pub. They stocked the bar in the hall and decanted wine into the carafes and by the time the forty traffic cops began arriving on the Friday night they were ready for them.

Some of the forty had obviously been in the pub during the afternoon and arrived in high spirits. By the time they were all assembled the hall was flooded with conversation and laughter. Arty and Joe, wearing ties, were kept busy dispensing drinks.

The meeting was called to order. They all sat down at the tables. The first of the dignitaries at the top table took the microphone and welcomed everyone to the convention and delivered a rambling speech about the camaraderie and cooperation among the members of this noble profession. There was applause. Drinks were replenished and a second dignitary arose and spoke at length about duty, dedication, responsibility, commitment, courage and courtesy. More applause.

In the lull that followed this Foxy headed off Arty and

his tray of drinks.

"I have to propose the toasts next," he said. "Can you get me a glass of water or something?"

"That wouldn't work," said Arty. "You're supposed to charge your glass from the carafe on the table between each toast. That's what they're there for."

"What am I going to do?" whispered Foxy. "I'm not going to drink any of the filthy stuff."

"You'll just have to pretend to," said Arty. "But you'd better make it look good. It could be regarded as pretty insulting, the Toastmaster proposing toasts and refusing to drink to them himself."

"What can I do?" Foxy was beginning to panic. "I know what toasts to propose, I've been reading up on it by the book, but what about all the drinking?"

"If I was you I'd take a little sip each time and top up the glass and hope nobody notices. Here, take one of these glasses of plonk with you and keep it in front of you to make it look like you're joining in the festivities."

Foxy took the glass of wine as though it was a hand grenade and returned nervously to his table with it. He blew into the microphone and the forty slowly settled down. Foxy spoke about what an honour it was to have been asked to host the Annual Regional Convention here in Matea. Then he unfolded a piece of paper and said, "It's an added pleasure for me to have been chosen to act as Toastmaster for this occasion. And so, gentlemen, I would ask you to charge your glasses and drink to Officer Brady, who, as you know, passed away in June of this year."

"Officer Brady!" and they all drank.

Foxy sipped, pulled a face and dribbled a bit more wine into his glass from the carafe in front of him. Then he consulted his piece of paper again.

"And now, gentlemen, I would ask you to charge your glasses and drink a toast to Superintendent King, who retires at the end of the year after thirty-two years' service."

"Superintendent King!"

Foxy accidently gulped a bit more wine than he intended and coughed a few spluttering coughs.

There had to be a toast for the Organising Committee.

"The Organising Committee!"

"Absent Officers!"

"Newcomers to the force!"

"He's overdoing it by the book again," Arty whispered to Joe. "He'll be proposing toasts to the moths hanging around the lights next."

Foxy didn't toast the moths, but he proposed toasts to everything suggested in whatever book he'd been swotting up on.

"Officer Ryan, who confronted a motorcycle gang . . . !"

Sip.

"The wives behind us, without whose support . . . !"

Sip.

"The decreasing numbers of drink-driving offences!"

Slurp.

"The police, without whose support . . . !"

Slurp.

"The success of this eleventh Regional Convention . . . !"

Slurp.

Foxy finally sat down believing he had finished, but then one of the others stood up and proposed a toast to Officer Fox for his untiring efforts towards making the convention such a success, causing him to have to sip some more of 'the filthy stuff'. And still he couldn't escape. People kept coming up to him and tapping glasses with him, toasting everything in sight. At one stage Arty saw him shuffle into a group with a half-full glass of wine in his hand. A bloke in the group automatically topped it up for him from a carafe he had in his hand. Foxy tottered off looking for somewhere to put it and immediately ran into three blokes who insisted on having a drink with him. Every time he managed to leave his glass on a table someone noticed he didn't have a drink and passed him a fresh one.

The dinner was served up and eaten and the tables cleared away, and the drinking carried on.

"We'd better keep an eye on Foxy," said Joe. "He's behaving as silly as a wet hen."

Arty looked across the room and saw Foxy lurch away from a group of men who were laughing at him. He joined another group and started talking excitedly to them. They were looking at him quizzically, grinning.

"He's drunk," said Arty. "Probably doesn't even know it. We'd better get him out of here before he makes a bigger fool of himself."

"You see what you can do about him," said Joe. "I'll hold the fort here."

Arty put his tray of glasses on a table and went over to where Foxy was. As Arty approached Foxy saw him and said, "Here's one of them! He's one of the worst offenders! Do you know what he's been doing? He's been . . ."

"Can I see you outside for a moment, Foxy?" interrupted Arty.

"What do you want to see me outside for?" said Foxy suspiciously. "I don't trust him," he added, turning to the others. "He . . ."

"There's something out there I think you should look into," said Arty.

"A traffic matter?" said Foxy, getting serious.

"Yes, a traffic matter."

"There's no end to it," complained Foxy, as Arty took his glass off him and put it on a table and guided him through the people and out onto the street.

"Now what's the problem?" said Foxy looking around.

"You are," said Arty. "They're all laughing at you in there."

The cold air had hit Foxy. He reeled a bit and steadied himself against a parked car.

"I think I'm coming down with something," he muttered. "I don't feel very well."

"I'd better take you home," said Arty, taking Foxy by the arm and leading him towards the carpark behind the hall.

"Nobody's taking me home," said Foxy, trying to pull his arm away. "I'm perfickly capable of taking myself home."

They came to where Foxy's Commodore was parked and he fumbled in his pockets for the keys.

"I don't think you ought to drive, Foxy. You don't look too good to me."

"You don't tell me if I ought to drive," said Foxy. "I've got authority over all these cars," he said, waving his arms around the car park. "I'm a traffik ossifer."

"I'll drive you if you like."

Foxy unlocked the car and got in and fumbled with the ignition key.

"You'd better let me drive you," repeated Arty. "You're a bit under the weather."

Foxy ignored him. He started the car, scraped it into gear and lunged around the side of the hall and out onto the street. He hadn't even turned his headlights on. He didn't make it to the top of the street. He ran straight into the back of the school bus parked at the curb.

Arty heard the crash and ran to the ute and drove out onto the street. Foxy's car was scrunched into the bus. He was sitting with his hands on the wheel as though he was still driving along. Arty opened his door and dragged him out and shoved him into the ute and took off with him. He couldn't see any witnesses around. The racket going on in the hall had prevented them hearing anything out there.

Carol was still up when he arrived home with Foxy swaying and muttering in the cab beside him. She came to the door in her dressing gown.

"You're home early," she said. "My goodness, that's Foxy! What's happened to him?"

"He's rotten," said Arty. "Give me a hand to get him inside. We'll get some coffee into him. He'll have to stay here tonight."

"Why? What on earth's happened?"

"He's pranged his car, and if they find him in this state he'll blow his licence and his job and everything."

They got Foxy into the kitchen and sat him down and made him drink two cups of strong coffee. He was shocked into obedience by this time and it was no trouble to get him onto the couch with a blanket over him. In two minutes he was asleep.

"I'd better get back to Joe," said Arty. "We can take it from here in the morning."

By the time Arty got back to the convention the standard of behaviour had deteriorated considerably. A bunch of the forty were doing handbrake wheelies in a minibus in the gravelled carpark. Inside Joe was refusing to serve three blokes who were banging their glasses on the bar and chanting, "We want beer! We want beer!" Two others were swinging on the stage curtains. An argument was going on between two groups across a table. One character with his shirt hanging out was standing on a table conducting himself in a spluttering rendition of the National Anthem. The function was fast becoming a shambles.

"They're getting out of control," said Joe. "The wine's run out, but maybe I shouldn't have tapped the third keg of beer."

"It's their grog," said Arty, "but the sooner it runs out the better. Whenever we get the chance we'll run beer down the sink until the keg's empty."

"What's happened to Foxy?" said Joe.

"He pranged his car into the school bus," said Arty. "I couldn't stop him, he was out of his tree. I took him home to our place. He's flaked out on the couch."

"What did you do that for?" said Joe. "We could have got rid of him for good!"

"I didn't think of that," said Arty. "The poor coot's in enough strife as it is. He'll probably get away with it, but our next job is to get this lot out of here before they get out of control altogether."

So they poured as little as possible into glasses and as much as possible down the sink. Someone fell off a chair. Someone was sick. Someone pushed someone else, who pushed them back and they had to be held apart. Someone put the minibus in the drain at the end of the car park and it took about a dozen someone elses to push it out. Several someones broke glasses. Someone was standing at the microphone delivering a speech that no one could hear because it had been turned off. Someone ripped one of the stage curtains off its rings and landed with a crash on a table. Someone poured the last of the gin and whisky down the sink, along with the last of the beer, and they were able to announce that the booze was cut.

"Foxy's been just about the best-behaved of this whole bunch," said Arty.

It was two o'clock in the morning. Everyone seemed to

have had a good time, and if anyone noticed that Foxy wasn't there Arty and Joe saw no sign of it. They got the last of the forty revellers out and locked the hall and went home, leaving the cleaning up until the next day.

Next morning when Arty got up Foxy was sitting on the couch with his head in his hands. Carol had given him a cup of tea.

"How's the head, Foxy?"

"What am I doing here?" croaked Foxy.

"I brought you here," said Arty. "You got sloshed and pranged your car. Don't you remember?"

"Vaguely," said Foxy, shaking his head. "Where's my car now?"

"It's probably still buried in the back of the school bus," said Arty.

"Why didn't you take me home to my place?"

"I didn't want anyone to find you before you sobered up," said Arty. "You can lose your licence for that sort of thing you know."

Foxy groaned, aghast at realising what he'd done.

"Why did you do that for me?" he said. "You don't owe me any favours."

"We all louse up now and again, Foxy. There was no need to make it look any worse than it needed to."

"How badly damaged is the car?"

"I don't think it'll be driveable. We'll go round after breakfast and tow it over to the panelbeater's if you like. The sooner it's off the road the better."

"I'll have to report it."

"No, Foxy. There's no need to go reporting things that don't need it. It's a minor traffic incident. No one's been hurt. You'll only clog the system if you go reporting things like that. What you have to do is take the car round to the panelbeater and file an insurance claim. They'll take care of the rest."

"The car's not insured," croaked Foxy miserably.

"Not insured? You? How come?"

"I never have accidents," said Foxy. "I'm a defensive driver," he added weakly.

"Well that's going to cost you a fair bit of what you've saved in premiums," grinned Arty. "Here, have some of this toast."

It cost Foxy over three thousand dollars to get his car fixed, and four hundred dollars for damage to the school bus. There were rumours around the town that Foxy had too much to drink at the convention and ran his car into the school bus, and someone painted THE FLYING FOX on the bus, but Foxy stuck to the yarn that he was pulling in to park behind the bus and his foot slipped off the brake onto the accelerator.

Foxy never thanked Arty for what he'd done, never mentioned it, but a subtle change had come over Officer Fox. He seemed to have lost his zeal. He started turning a blind eye to minor infringements. He let people off with warnings. He returned Arty's wave when they passed out on the road. He led the Matea Christmas Float Parade in his prowl car with his lights flashing and a blast on the siren every now and then, and the car full of kids from the primary school. He drove all the way to Danby and back one night to get some medicine for Cliff James' mother that hadn't come through on the bus.

The Sergeant reckoned that Foxy must have got a clout on the head that re-programmed him somehow.

Like most of the people of Matea, Arty and Joe still kept a wary eye on Foxy. He was still pretty hard on drinking drivers, but he wasn't pulling so many of them up these days.

You had to be doing something obviously wrong for him to stop you. Arty and Carol and Joe and Helen had Foxy round to Christmas dinner at Arty's place. He didn't see much humour in Arty offering him a glass of wine, but he actually seemed to be enjoying himself on lemonade. He didn't want to go home.

For the best part of a year Arty and Joe had no problems with Foxy. He made them pull into a paddock one day and off-load an extra half-ton of posts they had on the truck, but he didn't book them for it. And he'd warned Helen twice for speeding. A different Foxy, still almost as hard to like as the old one, but much easier to live with.

Then one day when Arty and Cliff James were having a yarn on the street Arty learned that Foxy was being transferred to a town up north.

"That's going to be a blasted nuisance," said Arty.

"What do you mean?" said Cliff. "I'd have thought you'd be pleased to be getting rid of him."

"No," said Arty. "Foxy's not too bad these days. I don't know, Cliff. We just get a traffic cop trained up and they take him away and give us another one to start on. It doesn't seem fair somehow. New traffic cops always try to clean up the district. They're a hassle."

"We'd be unlucky if the new one turned out as bad as Foxy," said Cliff.

"He's not likely to be as bad as Foxy was when he came here," agreed Arty, "but he's likely to be worse than Foxy is now. At least we know him."

"If you stick to the rules you shouldn't have anything to worry about," said Cliff.

"That's the trouble," said Arty. "The rules of a new traffic cop are always different from the rules of an old one. No two of them have ever been the same round here."

"They've got a job to do," said Cliff.

"We know that," said Arty. "It's how they do it that gets people confused. Look at Foxy, he's been here for two and a half years and he hasn't made a single friend."

"I thought you and him were getting quite matey."

"No," said Arty. "You can live with Foxy, but that doesn't mean you have to like him."

"That's too bad," said Cliff, "because there's a bit of a send-off for him at the Station on Saturday afternoon and he asked us to invite you and Joe and Helen and Carol."

"No way," said Arty shaking his head. "We've already been to one of Foxy's shindigs. I've got my reputation to think of."

"Tough luck, Arty," said Cliff. "The Sergeant promised him you'd be there and that you'd be shouting a few beers for the lads."

"The Sarge said that?"

"Yep. You'll no doubt be hearing from him."

Arty shrugged. "We'll be there," he grinned. "Wouldn't miss it for quids!"

DEJA VU
GNOMES
NOVELTIES
DEJA VU
GNOMES
NOVELTIES
OMES
VELTIES
DEJA VU
NOVELT
PAT TREMBETH

Gnomes?

The world turned round, and as the Turnbull Valley tipped away from the sun shadows fell across the little country town of Matea (pop. 1675). People hurried home from work. A car with one headlight turned into Mill Road. Lights came on in the houses. Darkness enshrouded Arty Brown's cluttered yard. Arty, sitting at the kitchen table, contentedly poured himself another frothy home brew, spilling some on Carol's tablecloth. The kids were in watching telly.

"Who was that on the phone, dear?" said Carol.

"Visuals Limited in Danby. They've had a fire that's gutted their warehouse and they urgently need to stock up on props. They need about five thousand dollars' worth of my stuff. They're coming out tomorrow to get the first load. They'll probably just about clean me out of stock."

"Well I never!" said Carol. "I must say I wouldn't have believed that junk of yours would ever have been worth anything to anyone."

"I always told you it was going to become valuable one day," said Arty. "I guess I'll have to start stocking up on stuff again. There's a line of plastic garden gnomes coming up at the auction on Wednesday. I might just go down and put in a bid. You never know when garden gnomes are going to come back into fashion."

"Yes dear," said Carol.